THE QUARE WOMEN

THE QUARE WOMEN

A Story Of The Kentucky Mountains

Lucy Furman

With a New Foreword by Rebecca Gayle Howell

FIRESIDE INDUSTRIES

1923 edition published by The Atlantic Monthly Press

2019 edition published by Fireside Industries
An imprint of the University Press of Kentucky

Foreword copyright © 2019 by The University Press of Kentucky
All rights reserved.

Editorial and Sales Offices: The University Press of Kentucky
663 South Limestone Street, Lexington, Kentucky 40508–4008

www.kentuckypress.com

Cataloging-in-Publication data for the 1923 edition available at the Library of Congress

ISBN 978-1-950564-03-3 (pbk. : alk. paper)
ISBN 978-1-950564-04-0 (pdf)
ISBN 978-1-950564-05-7 (epub)

This book is printed on acid-free paper meeting the requirements of the American National Standard for Permanence in Paper for Printed Library Materials.

Manufactured in the United States of America

To
MAY STONE
and
KATHARINE PETTIT
Future generations shall rise up and call them blessed

Contents

Foreword by Rebecca Gayle Howell ix
Note About the Book xix
   I. The Quare Women 1
  II. Taking the Night 15
 III. The Fourth of July 29
 IV. The Singing Gal 41
  V. The Widow-Man 53
 VI. Devil's Ditties 69
VII. The Funeral Occasion 87
VIII. Moonshine 101
 IX. The Danger Line 115
  X. Farewell to Summer 131

Foreword

I Am a Quare Woman
On Reading Lucy Furman in the Twenty-First Century

> Lucy Furman, though an avid writer of Appalachian literature, is overlooked by the literary world. Students of American literature may never hear her name mentioned. Worse yet, students of Appalachian literature may never realize there was a Lucy Furman.
> —Christi C. Leftwich

I am Hindman Settlement School's third writer-in-residence. The second was the celebrated modernist James Still. The first was Lucy Furman.

In 1907, five short years after our school was founded by May Stone and Katherine Pettit, Furman arrived in Hindman already an emerging writer of note. While living in Evansville, Indiana, where she worked for many years as a court recorder, she had published her first story collection, *Stories of a Sanctified Town*. *The Critic* (the day's *New York Review of Books*) lauded it for choosing "matter" over "manner" and for possessing "a due proportion of spirit—quite enough to make the tales artistically good, and to give the reader that sensation of fresh air in the mind which is perhaps the more valuable effect of good fiction." Not a weak debut.

But it was the two decades she spent at the Settlement—chasing children and livestock, hands in soil—that were her most prolific, yielding five hit novels drawn from her observations and notes about the Settlement's experiment in the well-lived life.

We often erase our historical women leaders by rendering them old. The popularized photographs and paintings of radicals like Ida B. Wells or Eleanor Roosevelt are of asexual matrons, made harmless by the providence of menopause. The common portraiture of the Settlement's founders is no different. Gray-haired and bent is how we still remember them in paintings and photographs, if we remember them at all.

I see them quite differently. What a wonder! These strong, smart, young women rejected the easy marriages their middle-class stations would have promised them, choosing instead a place and culture not their own, choosing to teach, to learn, to co-parent other people's children. When I walk across the Settlement School's grounds in my day-to-day, I cannot help but see them before me, each a lantern of a woman, weeding the vegetable garden or teaching subtraction to an attentive class or laying a quilt for the Sunday picnic that would give everyone a good rest before the new week's work took hold.

Pettit and Stone came to east Kentucky inspired by Jane Addams, the history-making founder of Chicago's Hull House. Hull House was America's first settlement house, offering the progressive vision that all peoples, regardless of class, deserved a high standard for living. This, Addams believed, could be achieved through equitable access to education, which should be rigorous and holistic. Hull House served the city's near west side, a European immigrant community, with a pedagogy rooted in what Addams called "the three R's"—residence, research, and reform. While studying students for the systemic causes of poverty, Hull House used its research to push for legislative reform, while also offering its residents an education weighted as equally to the liberal arts as it was to vocation.

As Addams writes in her canonical memoir, *Twenty Years at Hull House:* "I gradually became convinced that it would be a good thing to rent a house in a part of the city where many primitive and actual needs are found, in which young women who had been given over too exclusively to study might restore a balance of activity along traditional lines and learn of life from life itself; where they might try out some of the things they had been taught and put truth to 'the ultimate test of the conduct it dictates or inspires.'"

Her notion of renting a "house in a part of the city" became the integration of an entire neighborhood into her pedagogy, creating many of Chicago's first public services, including its first playground. The Hull House neighbor would be encouraged to imagine her right to a whole life, her right to access, from healthy childbearing and nutrition to enjoying some good theater on a Saturday evening. As David Brooks wrote in his recent *New York Times* op-ed, "The Jane Addams Model," "This was not rich serving the poor (Addams hated paternalism). It was rich and poor, immigrant and old stock, living and working in reciprocity, and as a byproduct bridging social chasms and coming to understand one another."

The possibility of Hull House came to Addams when she traveled to Europe with her first love, the activist Ellen Gates Starr, where the two saw the advent of the settlement movement in London's Toynbee Hall. Addams and Starr decided then they would found a similar house in the United States.[1] Unlike Toynbee Hall, which was a community center of, by, and for men, Hull House was of and by women, for all. Addams and Starr were members of the New Woman movement, or what is now called the first wave of international feminism. In America, these women led efforts to end lynching, secure women's right to vote, and normalize higher education and a pink-collar workforce for white women. In Chicago, Addams enacted feminism's idea that resources aren't best distributed by a top-down hierarchy.

First-wave feminists also shared a dynamic effort to challenge the cultural firewall that defined a woman as property, which, in the higher classes, often meant that the woman was treated as a kind of adult-child, for whom protection and provision were necessary, and for whom responsibility was an unfit burden. A common path of resistance was a leave-taking of the acceptable domestic sphere, and many who were well-heeled—like Addams, Starr, Pettit, Stone, and Furman—had the means required to make homes in the public sphere, working tirelessly to advance human rights as they also redefined family.

Even in this context, Pettit, Stone, and Furman were revolutionaries. Choosing to lead from within not urban but rural America, our founders and their fellow teachers were original trespassers of this country's rural/urban divide. Given all I know of the challenges met by those who still travel between these two Americas, I am not at all surprised that Hindman's founders were as transformed by Knott County as Knott County was by them. It is also not hard for me to imagine the conflicts of culture and class that surfaced in their sudden meeting. As one neighbor said at the time of the school's start, "Mixing learns both parties."

In our founders' first and best intentions, Hindman Settlement School was less a project of gentrification than it was an effort to draw resources from urbanity to stabilize rurality. In their historical moment, industrialization was happening to Appalachia. Extraction corporations, such as those of timber and coal, had just discovered the region's natural wealth and with such corporations came the money economy. Our founders, those "level-landers," traveled into Knott County to find a place almost fifty miles from the railroad with the express purpose of bringing the settlement movement to Americans who still thrived in the agrarian economy—and with hopes of providing their new neighbors the skills, resources, and wellness they needed to prepare for industrialization's blunt force. As Stone wrote for *The Wellesley College News*, "People need to be trained to meet that coming order so as not to be swept away or destroyed by it."[2]

What I find especially alluring about the Hindman Settlement project is this: our founders understood that our greatest hope lay in strengthening the agrarian economy, not doing away with it. To this end, they understood where they were at. To adapt the holistic pedagogy of Hull House for a healthy rurality, our founding instructors would need to become students, welcoming the land as their teacher.

In fact, it was the writer of this book, Lucy Furman, who became the school's first director of grounds, gardening, and livestock. It was a position she invented, one she carried out alongside her already robust formal duties as housemother to the boarding young boys. It really is something to imagine. Furman's was a slight figure: the pair of her shoes found in the Settlement's archive is not much longer than my hand (and half as narrow). Further, I find nothing that indicates she benefited from prior farming experience. But there she was, growing and putting up food, managing flocks and herds, building and rebuilding fences, planting orchards. Her boys, who were at once her charge, her farmhands, and her students, "learned by doing," rising by 5:30 a.m. to complete chores before studying for seven hours and working on the farm for four and a half.[3]

Self-sufficiency was the ethos of Hindman Settlement in those days, as it was for the Settlement's neighbors. I know my own grandmother and grandfather were two of those neighbors, living just one county over and by that same ethos, occasionally selling a hog for cash money but otherwise growing, sewing, and building what they needed and wanted. It's a different kind of life than the one I live, having been born to a certain ease by way of my mother leaving her homeplace and joining that pink-collar workforce at age fifteen. Rather than at toil, I spend my days reading and writing, thanks entirely to my mother's sacrifices, though I long to know what my grandparents knew, to open the almanacs of wisdom I let die with them. Furman, Stone, and Pettit dared imagine that a person could have both hopes. Their progressive pedagogy gave students the academic tools they needed to succeed in a larger world, while also providing them the same high-standard immersion in agrarianism needed to succeed at home.

However, anyone who has been in a dependent relationship with any piece of land knows that life is hardly pastoral. In their first years, eighteen students and teachers all lived in an open plank (read: very cold) house. When they finally moved into a log house, for which they spent years fundraising—and selecting the trees from which it would be built—a campus-wide fire soon destroyed not only their new home but also its library of two thousand books.[4]

As an educator, the earth is indeed a taskmaster. This excerpt from a 1907 newsletter, written by Furman, should give the reader a sense of the Settlement's regular lessons:

> Our troubles began at the very start. The fence all around the place was in a tumble-down condition. It had never been strong ... positively inviting the numerous hogs of the neighborhood to come in and visit. All they had to do was to root under the light panel a little, lift it up and enter. They strolled in and out at pleasure, helping themselves to our potatoes, corn, onions, peas, lettuce and tomatoes.... It seemed to me that day and night for weeks at a time I never had hogs off of my mind. I would get up at all hours of the night to run them out, and the little boys were kept at it all day. Of course we did what we could to mend

the fence by nailing slabs and old planks all around the bottom. . . . By this time, however, the hogs were persuaded that they had right of possession and were determined to enjoy them.

And that's before she describes the issues caused by the town cows jumping the fence.

Such ephemera demonstrate that the Hindman Settlement project fundamentally advanced Addams's ideals. As May Stone wrote in one of her letters, "We came to learn all we can and teach all we can." By coming to east Kentucky with the intention of strengthening Knott County's agrarian economy, our founders realized soon enough they had to fully participate in the land's exchange, ultimately creating a far more balanced interchange among neighbors than otherwise might have been. Hindman Settlement was not simply a stage on which the pedagogy performed, but a piece of land, an ecosystem, a cocreator of the school's curriculum and success.

The official histories of feminism often account for the movement's urban profiles but rarely even mention the many, dynamic, and diverse rural feminisms that created change throughout most of America. Among these large swaths of land, the self-possessed woman lived differently than she of urbanity. As the sociologist Wilma A. Dunaway writes:

> In a period when so many feminist writers are questioning separate spheres assumptions, recent scholarship often reduces women to a racially and economically homogeneous group who are confined in their homes. Not only do such popular culture claims ignore the realities of the lives of poor white, Native American, and enslaved and free black females, but they also ignore the few revisionist works that have emerged about Appalachian women's work and community roles. . . . To varying degrees, depending on their class and racial positions, antebellum Appalachian women engaged in a complex portfolio of agricultural and nonagricultural labors that defied separate spheres norms, including farm labor and income-earning labors within and outside their households.[5]

My own grandmother walked behind the plow, not my grandfather. No task was ever too big, too hard, or too heavy for my mother. There she'd be, right next to my father, lifting a piece of our diner's equipment, a hunk of steel that should have taken a team of men to lift. This difference—between the way I was raised and the way many of my girlfriends were raised—has come as a common shock to me. My mother gave me a level-lander's life and a mountain woman's back.

The Quare Women is Lucy Furman's thinly veiled documentary fiction of Pettit's and Stone's entrance into the Hindman community. When I read the novel, between the romance and feuds, I read a tale of two feminisms coming into nascent, reactive contact: two kinds of womanhood brought into a commerce of ideas and resources.

Those wonders, those strong, smart young women, making a home in a place and culture not their own—at best they were naïve about, at worst willfully blind to, the many clashes of class they would encounter and invoke.[6] As middle- and upper-middle-class white women, the Settlement's founders carried with them the cult of domesticity in which they were raised. While they rebelled against its requirement that they marry in order to be free of their fathers' management, they had not yet awakened to other allegiances they maintained. Their letters, newsletters, and journals reveal their confusion and frustration at not being able to acculturate mountain women to the obvious habits of "good hygiene" and desirable leisure that the middle class bestowed.

I can only imagine the frustrated letters and journals that might have been written by the mountain women, detailing the new neighbors who knew little of the most basic skills.[7]

Inside *The Quare Women* the attentive twenty-first-century reader will find a window into both struggles, as well as the spaces of compromise and equity achieved. Consider, for example, the scenes in which the quare women's refusal to marry is determined by Aunt Ailsie to be a mistake that needs fixing—and how gently the quare women let stand their awkward lack of interest. Consider Aunt Ailsie's relationship to Uncle Lot, that their marriage was no doubt patriarchal in its projection but matriarchal in deed. Consider that word of the quare women's arrival spreads not in print, not in church, but in the mountain women's underground network of trusted facts and assumptions. Watch for Isabel's refusal to betray another woman for the love of an exciting man. Watch for the showdown over what kind of a person is intended for cow milking, male or female, and the extreme discomfort that the conflict causes among all parties. Watch too for the gender-bending little boy Billy, who knows exactly who the cow wants to milk her.

From the time of its first publication as a serial in the *Atlantic* to the last edition of the bound book, *The Quare Women* was a runaway success. Readers loved Furman's ability to mix the high drama of local color with the documentary pulse of actual lived experience. Thanks to the novel's significant royalties, Furman bought a piece of land adjacent to the Settlement. On top of the mountain's rise, she built a house of her own, complete with a wide sleeping porch that overlooked main campus. She called it Oak Ledge. I spent my first year at the Settlement living on Oak Ledge, in a house next to Furman's, walking my dog by that old oak every morning and night. Her house still stands, now with vinyl siding, the sleeping porch closed in for a bedroom. That quiet, creaky shelter, Ms. Furman's trophy, was the childhood home of Albert Stewart,[8] and then, much later, James Still's last place. Today it houses Randy Wilson, a traditional musician who spent thirty years as an itinerant art teacher in the nearby public schools. After Randy, another of us will come and make a bed there, try to do a little good work.

In 1939, John Steinbeck released his leviathan, *The Grapes of Wrath*. In 1940, Mr. Still would publish his most famous novel, *River of Earth*. And, in 1940, *The Quare Women* would enjoy its last go. Thanks no doubt to the pain of the Great Depression and the Second World War, readers suddenly wanted realism, not adventure.

Almost a hundred years have passed since *The Quare Women* was first published in 1923. The industrialization of Appalachia has come and gone, come and gone, and gone again, and all around me, I see a nation of people afraid to make eye contact with each other, afraid to cross that urban/rural divide. But I also see my neighbors, and the Settlement, returning to our shared origins in farming. Here, in this historical moment, we are remembering the land, our land, that it has been with us all the while, caretaking and taking care to teach us the lessons we most need to learn. Maybe this is the exact right time for us to remember Ms. Furman, to read her with an eye for what else we might have forgotten.

Rebecca Gayle Howell
Hindman, Kentucky
June 2019

Notes

The epigraph is drawn from "Lucy Furman: An Outsider's Image of Appalachia in the 1920s," *Journal of the Appalachian Studies Association* 5 (1993): 135-41.

1. Addams and Starr would also direct Hull House together until their separation, at which point Addams assumed all duties. Later, Addams would help found the NAACP, the ACLU, and the Women's International League for Peace and Freedom. In 1931 Addams became the first American woman to receive the Nobel Peace Prize.

2. If only it had proven to be that simple.

3. The boarding girls, house-mothered by another instructor, were held up to the same rigor, working indoor duties.

4. And this was only one of many such blazes.

5. Wilma A. Dunaway, "Challenging the Myth of Separate Spheres: Women's Work in the Antebellum Mountain South" in *Women of the Mountain South: Identity, Work, and Activism*, eds. Connie Park Rice and Marie Tedesco (Athens: Ohio University Press, 2015).

6. Perhaps the greatest venue for these conflicts was the kitchen, as has been beautifully evidenced by contemporary scholars Elizabeth Engelhardt and Marcie Cohen Ferris. For much more, I recommend to the reader their two books, listed respectively: *A Mess of Greens: Southern Gender and Southern Food*; *The Edible South: The Power of Food and the Making of an American Region*.

7. Much has been written and published on the significance of these interactions, and scholars have discussed our founders as being everything from benevolent social workers to colonizers. I recommend the reader begin with Karen W. Tice and Deborah Blackwell, and then go from there.

8. Albert Stewart, who came to the Settlement when he was five years old, felt Furman was his true mother. The influence he took from her was deep; he would become known as the "patron saint of Appalachian writers," going on to found *Appalachian Heritage* magazine and the Appalachian Writers' Workshop.

The atmosphere of this story, its background, and even many of its incidents, arise from the author's connection with the Hindman Settlement School, in Knott County, Kentucky.

I

The Quare Women

Aunt Ailsie first heard the news from her son's wife, Ruthena, who returning from a trading trip to The Forks, reined in her nag to call,—

"Maw, there's a passel of quare women come in from furrin parts and sot 'em up some cloth houses there on the p'int above the courthouse, and carrying on some of the outlandishest doings ever you heared of. And folks a-pouring up that hill till no jury can't hardly be got to hold court this week."

The thread of wool Aunt Ailsie was spinning snapped and flew, and she stepped down from porch to palings. "Hit's a show!" she exclaimed, in an awed voice. "I heared of one down Jackson-way one time, where there was a elephant and a lion and all manner of varmints, and the women rid around bareback, without no clothes on 'em to speak of."

"No, hit hain't no show, neither, folks claim; they allow them women is right women, and dresses theirselves plumb proper. Some says they come up from the level land. And some that Uncle Ephraim Kent fotched 'em in."

"Did n't you never go up to see?"

Ruthena laughed. "I'll bound I would if I'd a-been you," she said; "and but for that sucking child at home, I allow I would myself."

"Child or no child, you ought to have went," complained Aunt Ailsie, disappointed. "I wisht Lot would come on back and tell me about 'em."

Next morning she was delighted to see her favorite grandson, Fult Fallon, dash up the branch on his black mare.

"Tell about them quare women," she demanded, before he could dismount.

"I come to get some of your sweet apples for 'em, granny," he said. "'Peared like they was apple-hungry, and I knowed hit was time for yourn."

"Light and take all you need," she said. "But, Fulty, stop a spell first and tell me more about them women. Air they running a show like we heared of down Jackson-way four or five year gone?"

Fult shook his head emphatically. "Not that kind," he said. "Them women are the ladyest women you ever seed, and the friendliest. And hit's a pure sight, all the pretties they got, and all the things that goes on. I never in life enjoyed the like."

Aunt Ailsie followed him around to the sweet-apple tree, and helped him fill his saddlebags.

"Keep a-telling about 'em," she begged. "Seems like I hain't heared or seed nothing for so long I'm nigh starved to death."

"Well, they come up from the level country—the Blue Grass. You ricollect me telling you how I passed through hit on my way to Frankfort—as smooth, pretty country as ever was made; though, being level, hit looked lonesome to me. And from what they have said, I allow Uncle Ephraim Kent fotched 'em up here, some way or 'nother, I don't rightly know how. And they put up at our house till me 'n' the boys could lay floors and set up their tents."

The saddlebags were full now, and they turned back.

"Stay and set with me a while," she begged him.

"Could n't noways think of hit," he said; "might miss my sewing-lesson."

"Sewing-lesson!" she exclaimed.

"Had n't you heared about me becoming a man of peace, setting down sewing handkerchers and sech every morning?" he laughed.

"Now I know you are lying to me," she said, in an injured tone.

"Nary grain," he protested. "Come get up behind and go in along and see if I hain't speaking the pure truth!"

"I would, too, if there was anybody to stay with the place and the property," she replied. "'Pears like your grandpaw will set on that grand jury tell doomsday! How many indictments have they drawed up again' you this time, Fulty?" she asked, anxiously.

Fult threw back his handsome dark head, and laughed again as he sprang into the saddle. "Not more 'n 'leven or twelve!" he said.

"They're about wound up, now, I allow, and grandpaw will likely be in by sundown. You ride in to-morrow to see them women!"

It was past sundown, however, when Uncle Lot rode up, grave and silent as usual. Aunt Ailsie hardly waited for him to hang his saddle on the porch-peg before inquiring,—

"What about them quare women on the p'int?"

Uncle Lot frowned. "What should I know about quare women?" he demanded. "Hain't I a God-fearing man and a Old Primitive?"

"But setting on the grand jury all week, right there under the p'int, you must have seed 'em, 'pears like?"

"I did *see* 'em," he admitted, disapprovingly. "Uncle Ephraim Kent, he come in whilst we was a-starting up court a-Monday morning, and says, 'Citizens, the best thing that ever come up Troublesome is a-coming in now!' And the jedge he journeyed court, and all hands went out to see. And here was four wagons, one with a passel of women, three loaded with all manner of plunder."

"What did they look like?"

"Well enough—*too* good to be a-traipsing over the land by theirselves this way." He shook his head. "And as for their doings, hit's a sight to hear the singing and merriment that goes on up thar on that hill when the wind is right. Folks has wore a slick trail, traveling up and down. But not *me!* Solomon says, 'Bewar' of the strange woman'; and I hain't the man to shun his counsel."

"I allow they are right women—I allow you would n't have tuck no harm," soothed Aunt Ailsie.

"Little you know, Ailsie, little you know. If you had sot on as many grand juries as me, you would n't allow nothing about no woman, not even them you had knowed all your life, let alone quare, fotched-on ones that blows in from God knows whar, and darrs their Maker with naught but a piece of factory betwixt them and the elements!"

Aunt Ailsie dropped the subject. "What about Fulty?" she asked, in a troubled voice.

"There was several indictments again' him and his crowd this time—three for shooting on the highway, two for shooting up the town, two for breaking up meetings—same old story."

"And you holped again to indict him?" remarked Aunt Ailsie, somewhat bitterly.

"I did, too," he asserted, in some anger, "and will every time he needs hit."

"Seems like a man ought to have a leetle mercy on his own blood."

He held up a stern forefinger. "Let me hear no more sech talk," he commanded; "I am a man of jestice, and I aim to deal hit out fa'r and squar,' let hit fall whar hit may."

Next morning, which was Saturday, Aunt Ailsie mildly suggested at breakfast: "I might maybe ride in to town to-day, if you say so. I can't weave no furder till I get some thread, and there's a good mess of eggs, and several beans and sweet apples, to trade."

Uncle Lot fixed severe eyes upon her. "Ailsie," he said, "you would n't have no call to ride in to The Forks to-day if them quare women was n't thar. You allus was possessed to run atter some new thing. My counsel to you is the same as Solomon's—'Bewar' of the strange woman'!"

However, he did not absolutely forbid her to go; and she said gently, as he started up to the cornfield a little later, hoe in hand:—

"If I do ride in, you'll find beans and 'taters in the pot, and coffee and a good pone of cornbread on the hairth, and the table all sot."

Two hours later, clothed in the hot brown-linsey dress, black sun-bonnet, new print apron, and blue-yarn mitts, which she wore on funeral occasions and like social events, she set forth on old Darb, the fat, flea-bitten nag, with a large poke of beans across her side-saddle, and baskets of eggs and apples on her arms.

The half-mile down her branch and the two miles up Troublesome Creek had never seemed so long, and the beauty of green folding mountains and tall trees mirrored in winding waters was thrown away on her.

"I am plumb wore out looking at nothing but clifts and hillsides and creek-beds for sixty year," she said aloud, resentfully. "'Pears like I would give life hitself to see something different."

She switched the old nag sharply, and could hardly wait for the first glimpse of the "cloth houses."

They came in sight at last—a cluster of white tents, one above another, near the top of a spur overlooking the courthouse and village. Drawing nearer, she could see people moving up the zigzag path toward them. Leaving the beans across her saddle, she did not even stop at the hotel to see her daughter, Cynthia Fallon, but, flinging her bridle over a paling, went up the hill at a good gait, baskets on arms, and entered the lowest tent with a heart beating more rapidly from excitement than from the steep climb.

The sides of this tent were rolled up. A group of ten or twelve girls stood at one end of a long white table, where a strange and very pretty young woman, in a crisp gingham dress and large white apron, was kneading a batch of light-bread dough, and explaining the process of bread-making as she worked. Men, women, and children, two or three deep, in a compact ring, looked on. Gently pushing her way so that she could see better, Aunt Ailsie was a little shocked to find that the man who gave way at her touch was none other than Darcy Kent, the young sheriff, and Fult's archenemy.

After the dough was moulded into loaves and placed in the oven of a shining new cook-stove, most of the crowd moved on to the next tent, which was merely a roof of canvas stretched between tall trees. Beneath was another table, and this was being carefully set by two girls, one of whom was Charlotta Fallon, Aunt Ailsie's granddaughter.

"The women teached me the pine-blank right way to set a table," she said importantly to her granny, "and now hit's aiming to be sot that way every time."

The smooth white cloth was laid just so; the knives, forks, spoons, and white enameled cups and plates were placed in the proper spots; even the camp-stools observed a correct spacing. There were small folded squares of linen at each plate.

"What air them handkerchers for, Charlotty?" inquired Aunt Ailsie, under her breath.

"Them's napkins, granny," replied Charlotta in a lofty tone.

"And what's that for?" indicating the glass of flowers in the centre of the table. "Them women don't eat posies, do they?"

"Hit's for looks," answered Charlotta. "Them women allows things eats better if they look good. I allus gather a flower-pot every morning and fotch up to 'em."

Soon Aunt Ailsie and the crowd went up farther, to a wider "bench," or shelf, where the largest tent stood. Within were numerous young men and maidens, large boys and girls, sitting about on floor or camp-stools, talking and laughing, and every one of them engaged upon a piece of sewing. Another strange young woman, in another crisp dress, moved smilingly about, directing the work.

But Aunt Ailsie's eyes were instantly drawn to the tent itself, the roof of which was festooned with red cheesecloth and many-colored paper chains, a great flag being draped at one end, while every remaining foot of roof-space and wall-space was covered with bright pictures. Pushing back her black sunbonnet, she moved around the tent sides, gazing rapturously.

"'Pears like I never seed my fill of pretties before," she said aloud to herself again and again.

"You like it then, do you?" asked a soft voice behind her. And, turning, she confronted still another strange young woman, standing by some shelves filled with books.

"Like hit!" repeated Aunt Ailsie, with shining eyes, "Woman, hit's what my soul has pined for these sixty year—jest to see things that are pretty and bright!"

"You must spend the day with us, and have dinner, and get acquainted," smiled the stranger.

"I will, too—hit's what I come for. Rutheny she told me a Thursday of you fotched-on women a-being here; and then Fulty he give some account of you, too—"

"You are not Fult's granny, he talks so much about?"

"I am, too—Ailsie Pridemore, his maw's maw, that holp to raise him, and that loves him better than anybody. How many of you furrin women is there?"

"Five—but we're not foreign."

"Why not? Did n't you come up from the level land?"

"Yes, from the Blue Grass. But that's part of the same state, and we're all from the same stock, and really kin, you know."

"No, I never heared of having no kin down in the level country."

"Yes, our forefathers came out together in the early days. Some stopped in the mountains, some went farther into the wilderness—that's all the difference."

"Well, hain't that a sight now! I'm proud to hear hit, though, and to have sech sprightly looking gals for kin. Did you ride on the railroad train to get here?"

"Yes, one day by train, and a little over two days by wagon."

Aunt Ailsie sighed deeply. "'Pears like I'd give life hitself to see a railroad train!" she said. "I hain't never been nowhere nor seed nothing. Ten mile is the furdest ever I got from home."

"Well, it's not too late—you must travel yet."

"Not me, woman," declared Aunt Ailsie. "My man is again' women-folks a-going anywheres; he allows they'll be on the traipse allus, if ever they take a start. What might your name be?"

"Virginia Preston."

"And how old air you, Virginny?"

"How old would you guess?"

"Well, I would say maybe eighteen or nineteen."

"I'm twenty-eight," replied Virginia.

"Now you know you hain't! No old woman could n't have sech rosy jaws and tender skin!"

"Yes, I am; but I don't call it old."

"Hit's old, too; when I were twenty-eight, I were very nigh a grandmaw."

"You must have married very young."

"No, I were fourteen. That hain't young—my maw, she married at twelve, and had sixteen in family. I never had but a small mess of young-uns,—eight,—and they're all married and gone, or else dead, now, and me and Lot left alone. Where's your man while you traveling the country this way?"

"I have no man—I'm not married."

"What?" demanded Aunt Ailsie, as if she could not have heard aright.

"I have no husband—I am not married," repeated the stranger.

Aunt Ailsie stared, dumb, for some seconds before she could speak. "Twenty-eight, and hain't got a man!" she then exclaimed. She looked Virginia all over again, as if from a new point of view, and with a gaze in which curiosity and pity were blended. "I never in life seed but once old maid before, and she was fittified," she remarked tentatively.

"Well, at least I don't have fits," laughed Virginia.

Lost in puzzled thought, Aunt Ailsie turned to the books. "What did you fotch them up here for?" she asked.

"For people to read and enjoy."

"They won't do me no good,"—with a sigh,—"nor nobody else

much. I hain't got nary grain of larning, and none of the women-folks hain't got none to speak of. But a few of the men-folks they can read: my man, he can,"—with pride,—"and maybe some of the young-uns."

A collection of beautifully colored sea-shells next claimed her attention; and then Virginia adjusted a stereopticon before her eyes, and for a long time she was lost in wonderful sights. At last, when she was again conscious of her surroundings, her eyes fell upon Fult's dark head near-by, close to Aletha Lee's fair one, both bent over pieces of sewing, while Lethie's baby brother, her constant charge, played on the floor between them.

"If there hain't my Fulty, jest like he said," she exclaimed joyfully. "And I made sure he was lying to me. Hit shore is a sight for sore eyes, to see him with sech a harmless weepon in hand! Does he behave hisself that civil all the time?"

"Yes, indeed—always."

A sudden cloud fell upon Aunt Ailsie's face. "As I come up," she said, "I seed Darcy Kent there in the cook's house. Hit would n't never do for him and Fulty to meet here on the hill. They hain't hardly met for two year without gun-play."

"Oh, I'm sure they'd never do such things in our presence!"

"Don't you be too sure, woman," admonished Aunt Ailsie. "There is sech feeling betwixt them boys, they hain't liable to stop for nothing. For twenty-five year their paws fit,—the war betwixt Fallons and Kents has gone on nigh thirty year now,—and they hate each other worse 'n pizen. I raised Fulty myself, mostly, hoping he never would foller in the footsteps of Fighting Fult, his paw. And he never, neither, till Fighting Fult was kilt by Rafe Kent, Darcy's paw, four year gone. Then, of course, hit was laid on him, you might say, to revenge his paw—being the first born, and the rest mostly gals,—and the day he were eighteen he rid right out in the open and shot Rafe in the heart—the Fallons never did foller laywaying. And of course the jury felt for him and give him jest a light sentence—five year. And then the Governor pardoned him out atter one year. And then he fit in Cuby nigh a year. Then, when he come back home, hit wa'n't no time till him and Darcy was a-warring nigh as bad as their paws had been; and for two year we hain't seed naught but trouble, and I have looked every day for Fulty to be fotched in dead."

"Yes, Uncle Ephraim told us about the feud between them. It is very sad, when both are such fine young men."

There was a stir among the young folks, who rose, put away their work, and gathered at one end of the tent, under the big flag. Then the strange woman who had taught them sewing sat down before a small box and began to play a tune.

"Is there music in that-air cupboard?" asked Aunt Ailsie, astonished.

"It is a baby-organ we brought with us," explained Virginia.

"And who's that a-picking on hit?"

"Amy Scott, my best friend."

"How old is she?"

"About my age."

"She's got a man, sure, hain't she?"

"No."

"What—as fair a woman as her—and with that friendly smile?"

"No."

The anxious, puzzled look again fell upon Aunt Ailsie's face.

Then a song was started up, in which all the young folks joined with a will. It was a new kind of singing to Aunt Ailsie,—rousing and tuneful,—very different from the long-drawn hymns, or the droning ancient ballads, she had loved in her young days.

"They are getting ready for our Fourth of July picnic next Wednesday," said Virginia.

"I follered singing when I were young," Aunt Ailsie said after a period of delighted listening. "I could very nigh sing the night through on song-ballats."

"That's where Fult must have learned the ones he sings so well," cried Virginia. "You must sing some for us, this very day."

Aunt Ailsie raised her hands. "Me sing!" she said; "woman, hit would be as much as my life is worth to sing a song-ballat now; I hain't dared to raise nothing but hime-tunes sence Lot j'ined."

"Since when?"

"Sence my man, Lot, got religion and j'ined. He allows now that song-ballats is jest devil's ditties, and won't have one raised under his roof. When Fulty he wants me to larn him a new one, we have to go clean up to the top of the ridge and a little grain on yan side, before

I dairst lift my voice."

A little later Aunt Ailsie was taken by her new friend to see the two bedroom tents, with their white cots and goods-box washstands; and then to the top of the spur, where, in an almost level space under the trees, a large ring of tiny children circled and sang around another strange young woman.

"The least ones!" exclaimed Aunt Ailsie. "What a love-lie sight! I never heard of larning sech as them nothing before. And if there hain't Cynthy's leetle John Wes, God bless hit!" as a dark-eyed, impish-looking four-year-old went capering by. "Hit were borned the very day hit's paw got kilt—jest atter Cynthy got the news. I tell you, Virginny, hit were a sorry time for her—left a widow-woman with seven young-uns, mostly gals."

"Little John Wes is very bright and attractive."

"Hit is that—and friendly, too; hit never sees a stranger!"

"He gives us a good deal of trouble, though, with his smoking and chewing."

"Yes, hit's pyeert every way; I hain't seed hit for a year or two without a chaw in hit's jaw. And liquor! Hit's a sight the way that young-un can drink. Fulty and t'other boys they jest load him up, to see the quare things he'll do."

At this moment the little kindergartners were dismissed, and marched, as decorously as they were able, down the hill after their teacher, followed by all the onlookers. The tents were discharging their crowds, too, and Aunt Ailsie recognized several more of her grandchildren on the way down.

Arrived at the lowest tent, Aunt Ailsie presented her baskets of apples and eggs to the women. A dozen or more elderly folk, and as many young girls who were deeply interested in learning "furrin" cooking, remained to dinner. The rest of the strange women, Amy, the kindergartner, the cooking teacher and the nurse, Aunt Ailsie now met, putting to each the inevitable questions as to name, age, and condition of life. As each smilingly replied that she had no man, a cloud of real distress gathered on Aunt Ailsie's brow, which not all the novel accompaniments of the meal could entirely banish.

Afterward, when the dishes were washed and all sat around in groups under the trees, resting, she said confidentially to Virginia:—

"I am plumb tore up in my mind over you women, five of you, and as good-lookers as ever I beheld, and with sech nice, common ways, too, not having no man. Hit hain't noways reasonable. Maybe the men in your country does a sight of fighting, like ourn, and has been mostly kilt off?"

"No, we have no feuds or fighting down there—there are plenty of men."

"Well, what's wrong with 'em, then? Hain't they got no feelings—to let sech a passel of gals get past 'em? That-air cook, now,—her you call Annetty, with the blue eyes and crow's-wing hair, and not but twenty-three; now what do you think about men-folks that would let her live single?"

"Maybe they can't help themselves," laughed Virginia; "maybe she does n't want to marry."

"Not want to marry? Everybody does, don't they?"

"Did you?"

"I did, too. My Lot was as pretty a boy as ever rid down a creek—jest pine-blank like Fulty."

"And you've never been sorry for it?"

"Nary a day." Then she caught her breath, leaned forward, and spoke in Virginia's ear: "Nary a day till he j'ined! I allus was gayly-like and loved to sing song-ballats, and get about, and sech; and my ways don't pleasure him none sence then, and hit's hard to ricollect and not rile him. But, woman, while I've got the chanct, I want to ax you one more thing, for I know hit's the first question my man will put when I get home. How come you furrin women to come in here, and what are you aiming to do?"

"We came because Uncle Ephraim Kent asked us," was the reply. "A lot of women from down in the state—the State Federation of Women's Clubs—sent us up to Perry County last summer, to see what needed to be done for the young people of the mountains. And one day, while we were there, Uncle Ephraim walked over and made us promise to come to the Forks of Troublesome if we ever returned. And we are here to learn all we can, and teach all we can, and make friends, and give the young folks something pleasant to do and to think about. But here comes Uncle Ephraim up the hill: he'll tell you more about it."

An impressive figure was approaching—that of a tall, thin old man, with smooth face, fine dark eyes, and a mane of white hair, uncovered by a hat, wearing a crimson-linsey hunting-jacket, linen homespun trousers, and moccasins, and carrying a long staff. Amy, who had joined him, brought him over to the bench where Virginia and Aunt Ailsie were sitting.

"Well, how-dye, Uncle Ephraim, how do you find yourself?" was Aunt Ailsie's greeting.

"Fine, Ailsie—better, body and sperrit, than ever I looked to be."

"I allow you done a good deed when you fotched these furrin women in."

"I did, too, the best I ever done," he said, with conviction. Sitting down, he looked out over the valley of Troublesome, the village below, and the opposite steep slopes. "You know how things has allus been with us, Ailsie, shut off in these rugged hills for uppards of a hunderd year, scarce knowing there was a world outside, with nobody going out or coming in, and no chance ever for the young-uns to get larning or manners. When I were jest a leetle chunk of a shirt-tail boy, hoeing corn on yon hill-sides,"—pointing to the opposite mountain,—"I would look up Troublesome, and down Troublesome, and wonder if anybody would ever come in to larn us anything. And as I got older, I follered praying for somebody to come. I growed up; nobody come. My offsprings, to grands and greats, growed up; still nobody come. And times a-getting wusser every day, with all the drinking and shooting and wars and killings—as well you know, Ailsie."

"I do, too," sighed Aunt Ailsie.

"Then last summer, about the time the crap was laid by, I heared how some strange women had come in and sot up tents over in Perry, and was a-doing all manner of things for young-uns. And one day I tuck my foot in my hand,—though I be eighty-two, twenty mile still hain't no walk for me,—and went acrost to see 'em. Two days I sot and watched them and their doings. Then I said to 'em, 'Women, my prayers is answered. You air the ones I have looked for for seventy year—the ones sont in to help us. Come next summer to the Forks of Troublesome and do what the sperrit moves you for my grands and greats and t'other young-uns that needs hit.' And here they be, doing not only for the young, but for every age. And there hain't been a gun shot off in town sence the first night they come in. And all hands is a-larning civility and God-fearingness."

"Yes, and Fulty and his crowd sets up here and sews every morning."

"And that hain't all. I allow you won't hardly believe your years, when I tell you that I'm a-getting me larning." He drew a new primer from his pocket, and held it out to her with pride. "Already, in three lessons, Amy here has teached me my letters, and I am beginning to spell. And I will die a larned man yet, able to read in my grandsir's old Bible!"

Aunt Ailsie was speechless a moment before replying, "I'm proud for you, Uncle Ephraim—I shore am glad. I wisht hit was me!"

But already the young people were trooping blithely up the hill and past the dining-tent. For, from two to three was "play-time" on the hill, and every young creature from miles around came to it. Fult went by with his pretty sweetheart, Lethie, whose two-year old baby brother he carried on his arm. For Lethie, though but seventeen, had had to be mother to her father's five younger children for two years, and would never let little Madison out of her sight.

The older folks followed to the top of the spur, and Virginia told a hero-story, and the nurse gave a five-minute talk; and then the play-games began, all taking partners and forming a large ring, and afterward going through many pretty figures, singing as they played, Fult's rich voice in the lead. Aunt Ailsie had played all the games when she was young; her ancestors had played them on village greens in Old England for centuries. Her eyes shone as she watched the flying feet and happy faces.

They were in the very midst of a play-game and song called "Old Betty Larkin," when the singing suddenly broke off, and everybody stood stock still in their tracks. The cooking-teacher—the young woman with the blue eyes and crow's-wing hair—was stepping into the circle, and with her was Darcy Kent.

All eyes were riveted upon Fult. He stiffened for a bare instant, a deep flush overspread his face as his eyes met Darcy's; then, with scarcely a break, he took up the song again and deliberately turned and swung his partner, Lethie.

Astonishment took the place of apprehension, faces relaxed, feet became busy. Aunt Ailsie, who had not been able to suppress a cry of fear, laid a trembling hand on Uncle Ephraim's arm.

"Hit's a meracle!" she exclaimed.

"Hit is," he agreed, solemnly.

She ran to Virginia and Amy, in her excitement throwing an arm about each.

"Do you see that sight—Fulty and Darcy a-playing together in the same game, as peaceable as lambs?"

"Yes," they said.

"I would n't believe if I did n't see," she declared. "Women, if I was sot down in Heaven, I could n't be more happier than I am this day; and two angels with wings could n't look half as good to me as you two gals. And I love you for allus-to-come, and I want you to take the night with me a-Monday, if you feel to."

"We shall love to come."

"And I'll live on the thoughts of seeing you once more. And, women,"—she drew them close and dropped her voice low,—"seems like hit purely breaks my heart to think of you two sweet creaturs a-living a lone-lie life like you do, without ary man to your name. And there hain't no earthly reason for hit to go on. I know a mighty working widow-man over on Powderhorn, with a good farm, and a tight house, and several head of property, and nine orphant young-uns. I'll get the word acrost to him right off; and if one of you don't please him, t' other will; and quick as I get one fixed in life I'll start on t' other. And you jest take heart—I'll gorrontee you won't live lone-lie much longer, neither one of you!"

II

Taking the Night

WHEN Aunt Ailsie returned from her visit to The Forks on Saturday, she gave Uncle Lot a full account of the strange women in the "cloth houses" on the hill—their names, ages, looks, and unmarried condition, and the activities they carried on.

"But the prettiest sight I seed, paw, was Fulty and t'other wild boys that runs with him a-setting there so peaceable and civil, a-hemming handkerchers. And the amazingest was Fulty and Darcy a-playing together in the same set, and nary a shoot shot."

Uncle Lot turned these things over in his mind as he sat on the porch after supper, gazing up into the virgin forest of the mountain in front. After a while he quoted:—

"'The lips of a strange woman drop honey, and her mouth is smoother than butter; yea, the furrin woman is a norrow pit, and they that are abhorred of the Lord shall fall therein.'

"I give you the benefit of Solomon's counsel, Ailsie, afore you went in to see them women; but you tuck your perverse way, and now you have seed for yourself. What made Fulty and his crowd of boys set there so mild and tame, with needles instid of weepons in their hands? What caused Darcy and Fult to forgit their hatred and play together like sucking lambs? Why, nothing naetural or righteous by no means—naught but a devil's device, a bewitchment them furrin women has laid upon 'em. I can relate to you right now what them women is, beyand a doubt. A body knows in reason that five good-lookers like them is bound to have husbands somewhere or 'nother; and my ingrained opinion is that the last of 'em is runaway wives that has tired of their men and their duty, and come off up here to lay their spells on t' other men. Which is as good as proved by what you have told."

Aunt Ailsie gasped. "O paw," she said, "if you was to talk to 'em you'd know they wa'n't that kind!"

"If I was to talk to 'em," declared Uncle Lot, judicially, "I'd examinate and cross-question 'em tell I got at the pine-blank facts of the case. I'm a fa'r lawyer myself, having sot on so many grand juries, and I would n't leave ary stone onturned tell I proved upon 'em what they air!"

After this, Aunt Ailsie dared not inform him that she had asked two of the women to take the night with her Monday night.

The following day—Sunday—Uncle Lot started off at daylight for a distant "funeral occasion," and she improved the time by giving her house a searching cleaning. She also swept the yard all around, under the big apple trees, until not a speck or a blade of anything was left upon it.

Then she walked up the branch half a mile, to her son Lincoln's, and said to his wife:—

"Fetch the young-uns and come down tomorrow early, Rutheny, and help me bake and get ready for company. I axed two of them women on the hill—Virginny and Amy—to take the night with me, and now I'm afeared I won't have things fixed right. And don't name nothing to Lot about their coming."

Ruthena and her four youngest came early in the morning (her other four were helping their father hoe corn), and all day a deal of cooking went on. As it all had to be done over a big open fireplace, there was some back-breaking work. When Uncle Lot came down from the field to dinner, traces of the preparations were hastily removed; but after he left, things proceeded again rapidly.

When it came to setting the table, Aunt Ailsie looked disapprovingly at her yellow-and-red checked oilcloth. "Them women had fair white linen on theirn," she said.

"Maw, them fine linen burying-sheets you wove thirty year gone, and kept laid away so careful ever sence—if I was you, I'd take 'n' use one of them. I will iron hit out good, and hit will look all right, and not be sp'ilt for buryings. And if I was you, I'd put t' other on the women's bed—I heard Cynthy's Charlotty say they follered laying between sheets instid of quilts and kivers, like we do."

"Yes, and they had fine linen handkerchers on their table, too, alongside everybody's plate,"—in a discouraged voice; "but I hain't got no sech. Minervy, you run out and pick a pretty flower-pot right off—they had posies in the middle of their table, and I aim to make 'em feel at home if I can."

Half an hour before sundown, the two guests, Amy and Virginia, arrived. Before sitting down on the porch, they must first get acquainted with Ruthena and her four little ones, and admire the pretty looks of the latter.

"And they hain't all I got," volunteered Ruthena; "I'm twenty-five year old, and got eight young-uns."

"And these here women is twenty-eight, and hain't got even a man!" said Aunt Ailsie, in a distressed voice.

"Eight is quite a large family, is n't it?" remarked Amy.

Ruthena opened her eyes. "Why, no," she said; "a body expects to have anyhow twelve, don't they?"

"Not where we came from," replied the guests.

Their attention was next drawn by the big loom that filled one end of the porch, and the two spinning-wheels, a large one for wool, a small one for flax, that stood near it. This led to questions about Aunt Ailsie's weaving, and to the display of shelves and "chists" full of handsome blankets and lovely "kivers" (coverlets). Although all her children had been freely dowered with both when they married, Aunt Ailsie still had many left.

"I have follered weaving all my life," she said; "hit is my delight, all the way along: shearing the sheep, washing the wool, cyarding and spinning and dyeing hit, and then weaving the patterns—hit is all pretty work. But best of all is the dyeing—seeing the colors come out so bright and fair."

The coverlet patterns were beautiful, but not more so than their names—"Dogwood Blossom and Trailing Vine," "Star of the East," "Queen Anne's Favor-rite," "Snail-Trail and Cat-Track," "Pine-Bloom," "Flower of Edinboro." A perfect one in old-rose and cream was pulled out and laid across the burying-sheet on the visitors' bed.

"That is my prettiest. I weaved hit when Lot and me were courting, for my marriage-bed. You shall lay under hit to-night."

From the large room where the "kivers" were kept, and which seemed spacious in spite of its three fat beds, its home-made bureau, chest, and shelves, several split-bottomed chairs, and a large fireplace, the guests were taken into "t' other house," the remaining large room, which held a dining-table, a cupboard, a bed, and an immense fireplace where the cooking was done. On the hearth were pots and spiders, and from the rafters hung festoons of red peppers and shucky beans, and hanks of bright-colored wool.

Then they made a round in the yard, beneath the apple trees, to look at the strong old log-house from every side.

"This here oldest house," said Aunt Ailsie, designating the kitchen-room, "was raised by Lot's paw eighty year gone. Lot, being the youngest boy, stayed at home with the old folks; and when him and me was married, he raised t' other house and put the porch in front and back. We have lived here forty-six year."

There was not a window in either "house"—only doors, back and front.

The interest of the visitors in the spinning and weaving, and even in the old house itself, Aunt Ailsie could understand, but not the delight they expressed in the scenery roundabout—the rocky branch, the cliffs and steep mountain-slopes in front, the precipitous cornfields reaching half-way up the ridges in the rear.

"I have looked upon creeks and mountainsides too long to enjoy 'em proper," she sighed. "Though maybe, if I was to get away from 'em, I'd feel lonesome-like, like Fulty did down at Frankfort. Hit was mighty hard on him down there."

The two women shuddered at the thought of the free, wild boy chafing for a year within penitentiary walls.

"And hit done him more harm than good, too; he's been more wild-like ever sence. But, women, whilst I ricollect hit, I feel to tell you afore my man Lot gets in, not to pay no notice to nothing he says or does. He follers Solomon's counsel about strange women, and hit's untelling what he may do or say when he sees you here."

"Hit is that," agreed Ruthena; "paw's a mighty resolute man."

"And he hain't heared the news yet about your taking the night with us," added Aunt Ailsie, anxiously.

Shortly after this, Uncle Lot, hoe in hand, and all unsuspecting, stepped gravely up on the porch, and stopped in blank amazement.

"Here's two of the furrin women, paw, drapped in to see us—Virginny and Amy's their names."

The two arose and put out friendly hands, which Uncle Lot inspected and touched gingerly. Then, hanging his hoe in a crack in the chinking, he passed on through "t' other house," to wash.

Returning, he seated himself on the porch at a safe distance, and after a dignified silence, began, with a cold gleam in his eye:—

"Women, I hear you come up from the level country."

"Yes, from the Blue Grass."

"Quite a ways from home you traveled?"

"Yes, one day by train and a little over two by wagon."

"Aim to stay quite a spell?"

"Through July and August, we hope."

"Like the looks of this country, hey?"

"We think it beautiful."

"Hit kindly does a body good to break away from home-ties now and then, and forget about 'em a while?"

"Yes, indeed."

"I allow you left your folks well?"

"Quite well."

"And they make out some way to do without you while you're gone?"

"Oh, yes, very well indeed."

"Hit's a lonesome time for a man-person to be left with the cooking and the young-uns on his hands. Mostly I don't favor women-folks traipsing over the world no great."

"Not if they have husbands and children to leave behind. Though," added Virginia, "even a busy wife and mother is better for a little change, now and then, and ought to have it."

Uncle Lot cast a sidelong, triumphant glance at Aunt Ailsie, and returned to the attack.

"Quare notions is abroad nowadays," he remarked, "and

women-folks is a-taking more freedom than allus sets well on 'em. Rutheny here, she never even stops to ax Link may she ride in to town—she jest ketches her a nag and lights out. Eh, law, and even my old woman is allus a-pining to see new sights, and werried of where she belongs at."

"Maybe she's stayed at home too long—everybody needs a change of scene occasionally. We should love to take Aunt Ailsie down for a visit to us in the Blue Grass when we go back."

"Women, I'd give my life to go!" fervently exclaimed Aunt Ailsie.

Uncle Lot started up, his features working. "Never whilst I draw breath!" he declared; "I don't aim to see my woman toled off from the duties she tuck upon her when she tied up with me, and ramping around over creation with a passel of—of—of strange women. Men in the Blue Grass may put up with hit,—may *have* to,—but I won't. Whilst I live, I'm the head of my house and my wife, and home she'll stay! And other women I could name would be a sight better off in their homes, too, with their rightful men!"

Aunt Ailsie hastened to pour oil on the troubled waters. "You know well, paw, that I hain't never in life gone again' no wish of yourn, nor crossed you ary time in forty-six year. And I would die before I would go again' your ideas. All I said was I would *like* to go with the women; but the rael thought was fur from me. And hit's about time now for you to go feed the property, so's we can eat and get cleaned up afore dark. I allow," she ventured bravely, "these gals will maybe take the night with us."

Uncle Lot glared fiercely upon the visitors, started to speak, struggled for a moment between the claims of indignation and of hospitality, and finally stalked off majestically to the stables, whence he did not return until summoned by a loud blast of the gourd-horn.

Link and the four remaining children had already arrived, and the supper, a most elaborate one,—fried chicken, fried eggs, string beans, potatoes, cucumbers, biscuits, corn-bread, three kinds of pie, and six varieties of preserves,—covered every inch of the table save where the plates were set. Though there was plenty of room, Aunt Ailsie and Ruthena refused to sit down, or to permit any of the "young-uns" to do so, the two men and the guests being "waited upon" first, while the eight children stood about, in absolute stillness, with eyes glued to the faces of the strange women. Even the "least one," not yet a year old, was still. During the meal, Uncle Lot maintained a stony silence; but Link was pleasant, and there was plenty of talk among the women-folk.

Aunt Ailsie snatched a bite at the second table, and then, their help in dishwashing being refused by Ruthena, the visitors accompanied Aunt Ailsie to the bars, to see the cows milked. Dusk was falling, frogs were singing, mist rolled along the narrow strip of bottom.

Returning, all gathered on the porch, while the soft darkness came on, and a bright crescent moon hung over the mountain in front, lighting up its mist-filled hollows. Amy was reminded of a famous scene in Scotland, and spoke of it.

"Scotland?" repeated Aunt Ailsie; "I've heared my maw's granny say hit were the land she come from. She said hit was far away, yan side the old salt sea, and she was four weeks sailing acrost."

"And now there are steamships that cross in eight days—mine did."

"Tell about when you crossed, and what you seed, and all about them far and absent countries," urged Aunt Ailsie; and the eight "young-uns," who sat around in the same breathless silence, could almost be heard pricking up their ears.

Amy told of her trip, while all save Uncle Lot hung upon her words. Once he asked, dryly, "And who looked atter you on the way?"

"One of my college chums went with me; we looked after each other."

He grunted unbelief. "Hit hain't in reason that any woman in her right mind would start off on sech a v'yage without a man," he said.

Amy proceeded with her narrative. When London was mentioned, Aunt Ailsie said: "I have heared of London-town in song-ballats all my days. Do you mind, paw, in 'Jackaro,' the gal's paw being a rich marchant in London-town? And there's a sight more where hit comes in."

"Some things are best forgotten, Ailsie," admonished Uncle Lot.

"These old ballads you used to sing were made in England and Scotland, hundreds of years ago, and brought across the sea by your ancestors," said Amy. "I wish that Uncle Lot could feel willing for you to sing some of them for us."

"None of those devil's ditties don't never rise under my roof no more," declared Uncle Lot, inflexibly.

"We have heard Fult sing a few," said Virginia; "he has a very good voice."

"Yes, and a good heart, too, women," asserted Aunt Ailsie. "I holp to raise him, even more than his maw; and though he hain't nothing but a grand, I loved him as good as ary child I ever had. And I allus hoped he would n't take up with them Fallon ways. Of course, blood is blood, and nobody could n't be Fighting Fult's son and not have some of his daddy in him. But until Fighting Fult was kilt, Fulty never so much as raised his hand in no meanness, or tuck any part in the war betwixt Kents and Fallons."

"How long has there been trouble between the two families?"

"Nigh thirty year now. Hit started way back yander, over a brindle steer, and kept on till all the Fallons and Kents, except Uncle Ephraim, was pretty well mixed up in hit, and all the in-laws on both sides, which tuck in a big part of the county; and a lot was kilt and a sight more wounded. Fighting Fult, he was the meanest man in all these parts, and never went out without three pistols in his belt and a Winchester on his arm; and Red Rafe Kent was nigh about the same; and both was sure shots. And every court-time, or 'lection, or gethering of any kind, hit was the same old story—one crowd riding into town, and t'other facing hit, and a pitched battle, and war and bloodshed. And Rafe, he was sheriff a big part of the time, and Fult jailer, and siege would be laid to the jail, and hit would be burnt down, and all manner of lawlessness, and no jury never dairst bring in no verdict, and times was terrible. And when the women-folks would see the nags dash into town and hear the shooting start, they would snatch their young-uns and crawl under the house, and the men that follered peace would take to the hills. And things never got no better till Fighting Fult was kilt off by Rafe, and Rafe was kilt off by Fulty. Then there was a spell of peace, while Fulty was down in Frankfort that year, and then another year fightin' in Cuby. But sence he come back, and Darcy has started up the war again, there hain't naught but trouble and sorrow for nobody."

"Tell hit straight, Ailsie," said Uncle Lot, sternly: "Darcy Kent never started up the war again no more than Fult, and not as much.

Fulty, he come back from Frankfort and Cuby, and gethered him a crowd of boys and started in pine-blank like his paw had follered doing—drinking liquor and riding the creeks and shooting up the town and breaking up getherings. And first court that come on, the grand jury indicted him for hit."

"Yes, and you sot on that jury and holp to," interrupted Aunt Ailsie, reproachfully.

"I holp to, and will every time he needs hit," declared Uncle Lot, firmly. "And Darcy, he was filling out his paw's term as sheriff, and hit was his business to sarve the warrant on Fult. And when he done so, Fult refused to give hisself up, and drawed his weepon, and before you could blink, both had shot each other, though not fatal. I don't say Darcy never had hate in his heart for Fult—naeturely he would, atter Fult had kilt his paw. But I do say he never started up the war again."

"You allus was hard on Fulty, and minded to fault him," complained Aunt Ailsie, in gentle bitterness. "Seems like a body ought to show mercy on their own offsprings."

Uncle Lot exploded. "Don't let me never hear no more sech talk! I am a jest man, and a law-loving; and anybody that does lawlessness and devilment, be they my offsprings or other men's, is a-going to meet their punishment from me. 'My kin, right or wrong,' has allus been the cry of this country, and hit's ruination. As for me, kin or no kin, blood or no blood, let the wrong-doer be punished, I say, and will say till I die!"

"If every man in our state had that strong sense of justice," observed Amy, "the reproach would soon be lifted from us."

"It reminds one of the spirit of the old Roman judge, who sentenced his two wicked sons to death," said Virginia. "I must tell you how I admire it in you, and how sincerely I agree with you."

Uncle Lot seemed to be overcome with astonishment at their speeches. "Women," he said after a moment, "you are the first people, women or men either, less'n hit is old Uncle Ephraim Kent, that ever upholt me in my principles, or tuck the measure of my char-*ac*-ter. The folks in these parts can't noways see the jestice in nothing their own is consarned in. Ailsie here has helt hit again' me every time I holp to indict Fult, or spoke a word again' his wrong-doing. And as for Cynthy, his maw, she won't hardly speak to me; and, though she is my offspring, is the bitter-heartedest and keen-tonguedest woman hit ever was my lot to meet up with. But for her agging him on, hit is my belief Fulty never would have rid up and shot Rafe that day he was eighteen, and the war hit would long sence have been forgot. Yes, the women-folks has holp not a little to foment the trouble and keep hit a-going. And when I see women that is able to take a right and a jest view, hit purely surprises me so I hain't able to express hit. But this much I can say, and feel to say, that I am downright beholden to you, and have maybe jedged you a leetle hairsh and onkind, being prejudyced in my mind again' strange women by Solomon's counsel."

"I told you them was right women, paw, from the start," said Aunt Ailsie, triumphantly, "and you would n't noways take my word for hit. But hit's a-getting along time for all hands to lay down; and whenever you gals feel to, say so."

They expressed their readiness, and Aunt Ailsie brought a stick of light-wood from the kitchen fire, and, followed by the guests, Ruthena, and the eight "young-uns," went into the big bedroom. One end of the stick was fastened in a chink in the wall, and Aunt Ailsie, Ruthena, and the eight settled themselves expectantly on beds and chairs. After waiting some time for them to pass out, Amy and Virginia began in desperation to get ready for the night. Sitting on the edge of the burying-sheet, they first took down their hair and brushed and plaited it.

"Now what do you do that for?" inquired Aunt Ailsie; "I never heared of folks combing their hair of a night."

"It feels better to sleep with smooth hair."

Then began the embarrassing experience of undressing before the fascinated gaze of ten persons. First, the gingham dresses came off, then night-gowns were slipped over heads and bodies, while further disrobing proceeded. The pieces of underwear, as they were handed forth, one by one, were eagerly examined by Aunt Ailsie and Ruthena.

"Never seed so much pretty needle-work in all my days," declared both. "But them stiff-boned waists, what air they?"

"Corsets," replied the women.

The corsets were passed around, with many exclamations of interest and surprise. "Pears like hit would be mighty trying to walk around all trussed-up that way," commented Aunt Ailsie.

But Ruthena was other-minded. "Maw, I aim to have some myself, right off," she said.

"Now, women, them shifts you have got pulled over your heads now—what is the reason for them? I see you tuck off the ones you had been a-wearing."

"They are nightgowns."

"I sleep in the same I wear of a day."

"We like to go to bed in something fresh—it is better for health."

"Never heared tell of that before. Do you allus strip off everything you wear of a day?"

"Yes."

"'Pears like you're a sight of trouble to yourself."

"I aim to make me a nightgown, maw, but I won't know how to make no pretty one, like them," sighed Ruthena.

"Oh, yes, you will; we'll show you how, and help you," said Amy.

The two, being at last undressed, knelt by the bedside to say their prayers. Aunt Ailsie tipped excitedly out of the door and clutched Uncle Lot's arm.

"You allowed them was wrong women, and runaway wives," she whispered, "Come watch at 'em down on their knees a-praying, as pretty as angels."

She drew him to the door, and he looked on, evidently much impressed. Once or twice he shook his head.

Then Aunt Ailsie and Ruthena took off their shoes and heavy, home-knitted stockings, and went to bed in the rest of their clothing; while the three least ones, being barefooted, turned in, just as they were, with their mother, and the five older ones reluctantly departed to kitchen and loft. Uncle Lot then sauntered in, threw out the stick of light-wood, and, shedding brogans, socks, and trousers, took his place beside Aunt Ailsie, all conversing casually meanwhile. Evidently the process of "laying down" was not regarded as one requiring privacy, or to be accompanied by any self-consciousness or false modesty.

In the morning, before sunrise, the guests were awakened by a blast of the gourd-horn, calling the men in from the stables; and jumping into their clothes, they washed their faces on the back porch, smoothed their hair, and hurried in to breakfast.

The table was again loaded with fried chicken, fried eggs, string beans, potatoes, cucumbers, biscuits, cornbread, three kinds of pie, and six varieties of preserves. Uncle Lot himself was almost pleasant. Aunt Ailsie took advantage of the thaw to say, when the meal was nearly over:—

"Uncle Ephraim Kent is a-getting larning, paw. Amy here is a-teaching him, and he is going through the primer fast, and allows to read his grandsir's old Bible afore the summer's over."

Uncle Lot nodded approval. "That's good work for the old man," he said.

"Paw," continued Aunt Ailsie, "the women allow I might larn to read myself; that I hain't too old or senseless—that is, if you was agreeable."

Uncle Lot considered deeply before replying. "Hit has allus been my opinion," he said, "that women-folks hain't got no use for larning. Hit strains their minds, and takes 'em off of their duty. Paul, he says, 'the man is the head of the woman'; and though I hain't got no great of larning, I have allus believed I was all the head-piece needed in the family."

"Yes, that is true—the man should be the head of the family," agreed Virginia. "But in another place, you know, we are told to search the scriptures; and also Paul says, 'There is neither bond nor free, male nor female, in Christ Jesus'; and it does seem that everyone, whether male or female, ought to have the comfort of reading the Bible."

"Well, there's something in that—I hain't never thought on hit in jest that light. I'll study on hit careful, women, and try to do jestice on all sides, and spend my opinion on you when I reach hit."

"We are sure you'll do what is right. And one more thing we want to ask you before we go—won't you come in to our Fourth-of-July picnic on the hill Wednesday? We've sent word throughout the county for everybody to come to a basket picnic that day, and we hope to have a pleasant time. But people tell us we are doing a dangerous thing, and running a risk; and it will be most desirable to have the presence of a law-loving man like yourself."

"Hit is dangerous," pronounced Uncle Lot. "There hain't no known way to keep liquor out of sech a crowd; and there never is a gethering without out drinking and shooting. And if the two sides was to meet there, hit's untelling where the trouble would end."

"We think that we're making things safe," said Amy. "But still, it would be best to have a man of your opinions and influence present."

"Well, I'll study on hit."

"Women," said Aunt Ailsie, "what is a 'Fourth-of-July'?"

"It's the day our nation was founded, a hundred and twenty-four years ago."

"The time we fit out the British, hain't it?" inquired Uncle Lot.

"Yes."

As Amy and Virginia started down the rocky, winding branch,—for they had to leave early to help with the work on the hill,—Uncle Lot turned to Aunt Ailsie and said, weightily: "Them women may be quare and furrin and fotched-on, but, in my opinion, they hain't runaway wives. And, in my jedgment, if Solomon was here, he would allow they hain't *strange* women, neither."

III

The Fourth of July

On Tuesday noon, Uncle Lot announced to Aunt Ailsie that he would go to the quare women's Fourth-of-July picnic the following day, and would take her along.

"Hit appears to be my duty, as a law-loving man, like they said, to be thar on the hill in case of trouble, which is nigh-about sartain to come, there not being hardly a gethering in two year, be hit election or court or funeral-meeting or what not, that hain't been shot up, and sometimes broke up, ginerally by Fult and his crowd."

"O paw, you allus a-faulting Fulty, and him your own grandchild, and the picter of you when you was young!"

"Picter or no picter, I hain't proud of daddying no sech, and don't uphold none of his doings. And if Darcy's crowd is there, too, which hit will be, with all the county a-mustering, then hit's un-knowing what the day may bring forth."

About eight o'clock Wednesday morning, the two started down the branch—Uncle Lot, a tall, grizzled figure in dark homespun and black slouch hat, leading, on Tom-mule; Aunt Ailsie following on old fat fleabitten Darb. Profiting by the quare women's example, she had discarded the hot brown-linsey dress in favor of an everyday one of blue cotton; but she still clung to the black sun-bonnet and light-print apron—inevitable badges of the respectable married woman.

When they arrived at The Forks, the one street was lined with nags,—they could scarcely find two palings to which to tie Tom and Darb,—and a stream of people was zigzagging up the steep hill behind the court house. Uncle Lot went on up, while Aunt Ailsie stopped at the hotel for her daughter, Cynthy Fallon, whom she found in the kitchen frying chicken, while three or four of the girls packed baskets. Cynthy was complaining:—

"Fulty, he allus has so many to feed, jest pine-blank like his paw—all them boys that runs with him, and then a big gang more he's sartain to ax to eat. I allow to feed anyhow fifty."

"You go wash and dress and I'll fry what's left," insisted Aunt Ailsie.

Half an hour later, the two started up with their heavy baskets. Cynthy, too, wore a black sun-bonnet and print apron; and from their appearance it would have been impossible to say which was mother, which daughter. If anything, Aunt Ailsie looked the younger, Cynthy's face being so lined and drawn from the troubles she had had as Fighting Fult's wife and widow.

The first thing they saw, as they toiled up past the deserted tents, was a tall pole, with the great flag which usually hung in the large tent flying before the breeze. It was set beside the flat rock, just at the top of the ascent, which the women had named Pulpit Rock. Beyond, on the level top of the spur, were numbers of seats made by laying saplings across logs; and here elderly folk and mothers with babies were tightly packed, while hundreds wandered about, or sat under the trees, or against the small, latticed grave-houses; for the spur-top was also a burying-ground.

The two women, Virginia and Amy, who sat on a puncheon-bench beside the rock, with Uncle Ephraim Kent between them, beckoned for Aunt Ailsie and Cynthy to join them. A phalanx of young people, whom Aunt Ailsie recognized as the singing class, stood beneath the flag, all wearing sashes of red, white, and blue across shoulders and breasts. Fult was in the front line, beside Lethie.

Aunt Ailsie leaned forward and said anxiously: "Lot, he's sartain there'll be trouble; he says some of the boys will get liquor, shore, and then—"

"I'm not very much afraid," replied Amy. She turned to little John Wes, Cynthy's four-year-old, who was perched on the rock behind her. "Tell Fult to step here," she said.

He came forward, looking very handsome, his dark beauty set off by the bright colors of his sash.

"Your grandparents fear drinking and trouble here to-day," Amy said.

Fult drew himself up. "I have give my word," he said, "not only that there won't be no drinking and trouble on the hill to-day by me and my friends, but that nary drap of liquor shall be fotched up here by nobody. Me and t' other boys have been scouting around all morning, meeting folks as they rid in, and going into saddlebags and coat-pockets, and warning all hands that we aim to have peace on the hill to-day if hit takes cold steel to get hit. And Charlie Lee and two more boys air still spying around for hit, whilst I sing."

This astonishing transformation of peace-breakers into peace-compellers laid Aunt Ailsie's fears. A little later, however, when she saw Darcy Kent, Fult's arch-enemy, come up with the pretty young woman who presided over the cooking-tent, and sit down not twenty feet from Fult, anxiety again awoke.

"Hit gives me a spell to see them two so nigh together," she whispered to Cynthy.

The latter cast a glance of cold, withering hatred at Darcy. "'Pears like he's trying to get him a fotched-on gal," she sneered.

But the programme was already beginning, with the singing of the "Star-Spangled Banner" by the class, Fult's rich voice leading. Then followed a prayer by Uncle Lemmy Logan, an Old Primitive preacher. Then the reading of the Declaration of Independence by Giles Kent, the school-teacher, and a song and march by fifty little kindergartners, who aroused more enthusiasm than any of the performers; then Lincoln's Gettysburg Address, read, somewhat haltingly but most impressively, by Uncle Lot. Then more patriotic songs by the class, and an oration, "The Founding of Our Nation," by Lawyer Nathe Gentry.

All had gone finely so far. Everybody was reassured by seeing Fult and Darcy in such conspicuous and peaceable proximity, and attention was rapt, even the scores of babies being quiet. Then, when everybody hung breathless upon the orator's words, and he was just launching into his peroration, three loud pistol-shots were fired in the immediate rear of the crowd. Instant panic fell. Women, without a word, seized their smaller children and scuttled down the hill like rabbits; men sought the shelter of trees, all save a compact group, headed by Darcy and Uncle Lot, which made for the scene of the trouble. Aunt Ailsie wrung her hands.

"I seed Fulty leave the singers a little grain ago," she said; "I'll warrant hit's him!"

It was. They found Fult bending, pistol in hand, over a prostrate young man. "Hit's Charlie Lee, my best friend," he said. "He helped me sarch all comers for liquor this morning, and then I left him and two more to patrol the hill whilst I sang. First thing I knowed, I seed him behind a tree tipping a bottle, and gethered that he was drinking some he had tuck off of somebody, and, knowing his weakness, I felt sartain he'd never stop till he was crazy drunk. I had give my hand to the women there would be no drinking on the hill, and there was n't but one thing to do—take hit away from him. When I come back to do so, he already had enough in him to be mean, and refused to give hit up; and when I tried to take it anyhow, he drawed on me. I seed then the onliest thing to do was to shoot the pistol out of his hand, which I done, scaring him pretty bad, and maybe grazing two-three of his fingers, but not hurting him none to speak of. Hit was the only way."

Sure enough, while Charlie's hand was bleeding profusely, it was found that there was not even a bone broken.

"Where's the fotched-on nurse-woman?" was the cry.

But she was already at hand, with a small first-aid outfit; the fingers were quickly bandaged, and Charlie, sobered by the shock and extremely shamefaced, was soundly berated by Fult for his faithlessness.

And now arose a dilemma. By rights Darcy, being sheriff, should have placed both disturbers of the peace under arrest. He made no move, however. A hand was placed upon his arm, and Uncle Ephraim whispered:—

"Don't do nothing at all; hit would start a battle that would never eend."

Then the old man stepped forward, and spoke authoritatively.

"Fult here deserves a vote of thanks from the citizens of this county for keeping the peace here on this hill to-day, and not having hit broke up by even his best friend. In the name of the people, and the women, I thank him."

He solemnly offered a hand to the boy, who took it, flushing.

Uncle Lot also stepped forward. "I hain't never in life seed you do nothing I tuck pride in afore," he said to his grandson; "but you done hit to-day when you went pine-blank again' your feelings and your friendship to maintain the peace."

He also put forth his hand, which Fult accepted as one in a daze.

In fifteen minutes the women and children were all back, relieved and smiling, and the lawyer was completing his peroration. There was then a slight pause in the proceedings, while everybody talked of the panic and its happy ending.

Then, very slowly, Uncle Ephraim Kent, a notable figure, with his mane of white hair, his crimson hunting-jacket, his linen trousers and moccasins, his tall, lean body very little bent by the passing of eighty-two years, mounted the pulpit-rock and faced the audience.

"Citizens and offsprings," he began, "hit were not in my thoughts to speak here in this gathering to-day, even though the women axed and even begged me so to do. I never follered speaking, nor enjoyed listening at the sound of my own voice, the weight of no-larning allus laying too heavy upon me. But sarcumstances has riz and sot up lines of thought that calls for the opening of my mind to you, and I will therefore do the best I am able.

"And firstways I will say how I rej'ice that them shots that brung fear to our hearts to-day was good shots, and not bad ones, fired to keep the peace by one that has too often follered breaking hit. And I'll say furder that, in my opinions, he never would have broke hit that first time but for old, ancient wrongs, done afore he seed the light: sins of the fathers, visited down on the children, and ketching 'em in a quile they can't hardly onravel."

The audience, well knowing that the old man referred to the killing of his son, Rafe, by Fult, and to the previous warfare between Kents and Fallons, listened breathless.

"But," continued Uncle Ephraim, "let me leave that sorrowful tale for a spell, and go back to the good old days when there wa'n't no sech things as wars betwixt friends and neighbors—the days when our forbears first rid acrost the high ridges from Old Virginny or North Cyar'liny and along these rocky creeks, and tuck up land in these norrow valleys. A rude race they was, but a strong, with the blood of old England and bonny Scotland in their veins, and in their hearts the fear of naught; a rude race, but a free, chasing the deer and the b'ar and the wild turkey and the Indian, tending their craps with a hoe in one hand and a gun in t' other; a rude race, but a friendly, banding together again' all foes, helping one another in all undertakings. Some of 'em, like my grandsir, the old cap'n, come in to live on land that was granted 'em because they had fit under Washington; t' others jest wandered in and tuck up what pleased 'em.

"Well, atter they settled theirselves in this rugged, penned-in land, then what happened to 'em? Well, right there was the trouble—*nothing* never happened. Here they was, shut in for uppards of a hunderd year, multiplying fast, spreading up from the main creeks to the branches and hollows, but never bettering their condition—you might say, worsening hit. For before long the game was all kilt off, and life become the turrible struggle hit still is, jest to keep food in our mouths—raising craps on land that's nigh straight-up-and-down, like we have to. And while a many of the first settlers, Like my grandsir, had been knowledgeable men, with larning, their offsprings growed up in the wilderness without none, because there wa'n't no money to send the young-uns out to school, or to fotch larning in to 'em. And the second crap, of which I was one, was wusser and ignoranter still, being raised up maybe, like me, eighty mile from a schoolhouse or church-house; and the third was wusser and meaner yet; and so on down to now, when they hain't no better, though there is a few pindling deestrict schools here and yan.

"And about the onliest times in all them years our folks found out there was a world outside these mountains was when the country sont in a call to fight hits battles. Then we allus poured forth, rej'icing—like when there was trouble again with the British, and we mustered under Old Hickory behind them cotton-bales and palmetty-logs at New Orleens; and then later, when Mexico got sassy; and then when the States tuck sides and lined up, you know how we fit through them four year—mostly for the Union; this here stiff right arm I fotched back remembers me of hit; then there's this here leetle war in Cuby, too, not long finished.

"All of which proves we air a brave and fighting race. And if the fighting had stopped with wars for our country, all would have been well. But, citizens and offsprings, hit never stopped there. You all know how, when there wa'n't no outside wars to keep us peaceified, there was allus them amongst us, for thirty year and more, that could n't take no satisfaction in life onless they was starting wars amongst theirselves.

"And right here you will say to me, 'Uncle Ephraim, begin at home.' Which is but true and just. For well I know the part my offsprings has bore in the troubles of this country, and that the Kents, which used to be a peaceable gineration, has come down to be a mean one. But, friends, hit never was with my counsel or consent. I have loved peace and pursued hit. But all in vain. War hit raged hither and yan; battles was fit all over the county; and here at The Forks many was kilt—three of my sons amongst 'em—and many a more wounded, and sorrow was brung to many hearts. Hit was not until Fighting Fult and my son Rafe was both kilt, that we had a taste of peace. Then, for a spell, whilst young Fult was down at Frankfort, and fighting in Cuby, we rested; and oh, what a joyful rest hit was!

"Then young Fult come back, and sad times begun again—not that I am faulting him for hit, for Darcy, being older, ought to have knowed better than to sarve them warrants on him in the first place. Hit was like throwing fire in gunpowder. In my opinion, if the boy had been let alone a spell, to kindly work off his youth and sperrits, he'd 'a' soon settled down. But he wa'n't, and the war hit flamed up again, and for nigh two year we have seed trials on top of tribulations. As I said afore, I hain't blaming neither boy—both was bitter-hearted from the family hate which they had drawed in, you might say, with their mothers' milk; both had loved their paws; both had lost them; revenge was naetural. But if ever a people was wore out with wars and troubles, we air them people; if ever folks yearned and pined and prayed for peace, we air them folks.

"Yes, many's the time, walking the ridge-tops, standing up yander on the high rocks, I have looked down on the valley of Troublesome and agonized in sperrit over hit, calling upon the God of Israel to send us help and peace. Many's the time, too, up there, I have dreamed dreams and seed visions.

"People under the shadow of my voice,—all you that the mountains has give birth and suck to,—you know what I mean. Though we air ignorant folk, not able to get much acquainted with God through his written Word, yet He hain't never left us without a witness; He hain't never failed to speak to our minds and our hearts. In the high, lifted-up places, gazing out over the green mountain-tops, with maybe the sun-ball drapping low in the west, and the clouds and the elements all a-praising Him in their beauty; or maybe of a cold winter's day, with the whole world white and the snow a-sparkling and the shadows deep-blue in the hollows; He talks to us, He shows us things that no level-lander don't know nothing about, or get no inkling of—visions, and dreams, and things to come. You have all, even the meanest, kotched a glimp of 'em. For we air a seeing people.

"And several times in sech visions, friends, I have beheld down there below, in the valley of Troublesome, all manner of peaceful and happy homes, where every man had his mind made up to let liquor and guns alone, and the women-folks tended their offsprings in the fear of the Lord, and even the young was too busy getting larning to be briggaty and feisty.

"I allow, moreover, that there is but few here that, in their better hours, hain't beheld and wished for the same. But how hit was to come about did n't appear. We wa'n't able to help ourselves, or bring about a change; hit was like a landslip: things had got too much headway to be turnt back. We needed outside help, but where hit was to come from, nobody knowed. But from the time I were a leetle shirt-tail boy, hoeing corn on yon hillsides, I have had faith to believe the Lord would send hit in some time, from somewheres, and have never ceased a-praying for hit.

"And in the weeks past, friends, sence these here women tuck up their abode with us, hit has appeared like my prayers was answered, my visions a-coming true. I hain't heared a gun fired off sence that first night they come in; I have seed the boys that ginerally drinks and fights and shoots (because they hain't got nothing better to do) all a-gethered in, happy and peaceable, singing and playing, and even sewing; and the gals, that is apt to idle and squander their time, taking joy in larning how to cook right vittles and dig out dirt; and the older folks likewise waking up to things they never heared of before; and me myself,—which hit don't seem noways possible, but yet hit is true,—me, that nigh a lifetime ago had give up all hope of ever being knowledgeable; me, with you might say both feet in the grave, becoming a man of larning. For the women here has already teached me my letters, and I'm a-studying on page three of my primer; and before the summer passes I'll be a-reading in my grandsir's old yaller Bible I have churrished so long, praise the Lord!

"In all which, friends, I see the hand of the Almighty. Hit is Him that has sont these women in to us; hit is Him that has led 'em along the rough way to our help; hit is Him that has answered my long-raised prayers.

"Now, the Lord having done his part so complete, and these here women a-doing theirn, what about ourn? Deep down in our hearts, don't we feel to do something, too, to help along the good work and bring the visions to pass?

"There is several things, citizens and offsprings, we can do if we so feel to. One is to treat these women kind and friendly, and incourage 'em to keep on; another is to send our young-uns in to take the benefits of what they can get. But the most demandingest thing of all for us to do, 'pears like, is to patch up our differences and troubles for the time the women air amongst us, and publicly agree on hit. I hain't got no differences or troubles with nobody nowhere, thank God! but some of my offsprings has, and this is what I am getting down to, right now. I ax my grandson, Darcy Kent, and likewise my young friend, Fult Fallon, that has already showed sech a fine sperrit here to-day, to step forrard here, whilst I lay the matter before 'em."

The two young men, startled, flushed, reluctant, came slowly forward, avoiding one another's eyes, and stood, some distance apart, in front of Uncle Ephraim, at the foot of the rock. The audience held its breath.

"I praise and thank you, boys," began the old man, "that in these past few days, for the sake of these women and the work they are doing for us, you have turnt aside from follering your feelings and have sunk your troubles out of sight. I was glad a-Saturday, when I seed you playing in the same set. I was glad when I seed you, and all the boys that follers you both, a-keeping peace on the hill here to-day. Hit is fine and honorable in both of you; and the only trouble is, we hain't got no assurance hit will last, and that your innard feelings won't bust out in death and destruction maybe the next minute. Hit is, therefore, my desire to counsel you two boys—being the leaders in the war—to declare here and now a truce, a solemn truce, in the presence of this county, for the full time the women stays with us.

"Hatred is long and lasty, boys—you have got a lifetime before you to work hit out in. The folks of this county is plumb wore to a frazzle with fighting and fear. What they need is a spell of rest. I allow you would have kept the peace anyhow for these few weeks, out of respect to the women; but everybody'll feel better if hit's agreed on in public. Now I don't ax you to take one another's hands—hit would be hy-pocrisy, your feelings being what they air; but I do ax you both to jine hands with me, and give your solemn word not to take up the war again in no way, or let it be tuck up by your friends, while these women stays with us. Ponder hit, boys,—study on hit,—take all the time you need; be plumb satisfied in your minds."

Silence fell, while Uncle Ephraim and all the audience gazed upon the two tall young men, one so fair, one so dark, both so handsome, and both standing as if turned to stone.

Uncle Ephraim's voice again broke the intense stillness.

"As I look upon you two boys," he said, "both so pretty, both so upstanding and brave, both orphants through this war that has been handed down to you, both honest as the day, both feeling hit your bounden duty to kill each other off if you can, both knowing that, if either one had his way, t' other's fair body would be laying under the sod, hit does seem like sorrow plumb swallows me up, and my heart swells too big for hits socket, like I would gladly pour out my life here before you, if hit could only bring you together in right feeling.

"Boys, when Amy here was a-reading Scripter to me a-Sunday, she read where hit said, 'Give place to wrath—vengeance is mine, saith the Lord'; and another, and better, read: 'Love your enemies, pray for them that despitefully use you.' I ax you to meditate on them words in days to come, to open up your hearts and your minds to 'em. Not now,—the day is still far off when you can accept sech idees,— love being a puny-growing and easy-killed plant. I don't ax for nothing of that kind now. All I request is your word calling a truce while the women stays. All I ax is for you to think about the county and forget yourselves. Do you, Darcy, my offspring, and the oldest of the two, feel to give me your hand on hit?"

Darcy, flushed and then pale, reached up and slowly laid a hand in his grandfather's. "I do," he said, firmly.

Fult did not wait to be asked. "Me, too," he said, taking Uncle Ephraim's other hand. Then, impulsively, "And I'll say furder, Uncle Ephraim, that if all the Kents was like you there never would have been no war."

"There would not," repeated Uncle Ephraim, emphatically, clasping the hands of the two.

He looked out over the assembly. "Citizens of this county," he said, "you have witnessed this solemn covenant this day made and sealed in your presence. And I call upon all here that has ever tuck sides or had hard feelings, to see to hit that they keep the truce their leaders has agreed on, and make hit stand. And I hereby declare peace in this county for the time these women stays with us. And now, may the Lord dig round our hearts with the mattock of his love, till the roots goes to spreading, and the sap goes to rising, and the leaves buds out, and the blossoms of love and righteousness shoots forth and abounds in all our lives!"

IV

The Singing Gal

It was not until the train pulled out of the station that Isabel felt sure she was really going to the mountains. When the letter had come the day before, from Amy Scott to Mrs. Gwynne, begging the loan of her daughter for a few weeks, to help in the social work on Troublesome Creek,—"for," it read, "the singing classes are by far our most popular feature, and none of us can sing; our need of a singer is really desperate,"—Mrs. Gwynne had at first refused point-blank to let Isabel go. "I could not sleep at night," she said, "with you up in that wild country, where they do nothing but make moonshine whiskey and kill each other off in those horrible feuds."

Mr. Gwynne's persuasion, added to Isabel's importunity, had at last won a reluctant consent; but during the hurried preparations, Isabel was in constant fear of its withdrawal; and while she and her father were driving the three miles to town in the family carriage, she was haunted by the dread of galloping hoofs behind, and the voice of one of the negro boys at the window saying, "Miss Millicent say she done change her mind, and for Miss Isabel to come on back home." Even at the station, she was in such nervous fear that she could hardly show appreciation of Thomas Vance's presence, and of the inevitable box of candy and new novel.

She hardly knew what Thomas and her father said as they got her settled in the dingy day-coach (there was nothing better on this newly built road to the coal-fields in the edge of the mountains), her one desire being to hear the train-bell ring for a start. After what seemed a long time, it did so; Thomas and Mr. Gwynne jumped off, and Isabel felt that she was embarked upon the adventure of her life.

The trip was an all-day one, the heat great, the train exceedingly dirty; but Isabel was all eyes and interest. They passed, first, through the beautiful Blue Grass country, with its smooth, rolling pastures, clear brooks, sleek herds of cattle and horses, and stately homes like her own, set back amid tall trees; then into the poorer and rougher "knobs," where life was evidently a different proposition; then the knobs rose into hills, and the hills became steeper and higher, until the train was shut in between cliffs and mountains. The progressive change in the people who got into and off the train all along the way was as striking as the changing topography. It was hard to believe that all could belong to the same state.

About five in the afternoon they arrived at the end of the railroad—a mountain county-seat famous for the terrible feud then raging.

A tall old man in a slouch hat was standing by the platform, and as Isabel descended he inquired solemnly, "Is this the singing gal?"

"Yes; and of course you're Uncle Adam Howard," she answered.

Without a word, he took her suitcase and led the way along the track, between endless piles of ties and lumber. Once she broke the silence to ask, "How is the feud coming on now?"

To her surprise, he stopped, looked hastily all about, and replied in a low voice, "Hit hain't safe to talk about the war in public. Walls, and even lumber-piles, has years, and trees has tongues, and a man that aims to live peaceable can't see, hear, nor tell nothing."

He left the track at last, and turned up a slope toward an ugly frame house, backed into a cliff, which had the words "Mountainside Hotel" in large letters across its front. From its porch, a view of the straggling, muddy town could be had.

The loud supper-bell rang as they entered, and they went at once to the dining-room. Two drummers were the only other guests; the landlady and her daughters waited on the table, and the meal was a silent one.

When she was shown to her room afterward, however, Isabel ventured to make inquiries about the "war," and the landlady became loquacious upon the subject, and even offered to take her to see the blood-spots where several of the feudists had perished—an offer instantly accepted.

Skirting numerous deep mud-holes, and many reposing hogs

and cows, they came at last to the courthouse, stronghold of the law, which proved to be the scene of the blood-spots. There they were, on step and walls, black and grisly.

"Hit's a sight in this world, the terrible things that goes on, and the men that's kilt and wounded," said the landlady. "If my man was alive, or my gals was boys, I would n't never see ary grain of peace."

Just across the street from the courthouse, she pointed out the large store belonging to one of the feud leaders, from the upper windows of which the shots had been fired that caused some of the spots. "Laywayings," "ambushings," battles, murder, and sudden death, seemed to be the order of the day; and apparently neither the state militia nor any other power could quell the trouble.

On their return to the hotel, Isabel found in her room, which was also the parlor, the three daughters of the house and the two drummers. One of the girls was producing loud discords on an organ with a front of scrollwork over red flannel, which adorned one corner; and as she had preëmpted the only chair in the room, the others sat on the two beds.

After a long hour of this, Isabel was left in possession, and proceeded to make herself ready for the night. The bed-covers were very dingy, and, turning them back, she found that there was but one sheet on each bed, and it was far from fresh; so were the pillow-cases. She was dismayed for only a moment, however: opening the newspapers her father had provided her with, she covered the top of one bed, and then lay down on it, with her blue silk kimono and her raincoat for covers.

At earliest dawn she was awakened by Uncle Adam's loud rap, and the summons, "Get up along, sis; we got to take a soon start!"

After they had pulled through the deep mudholes in the town, they turned into a creek-bed, and plunged at once into a world of green loneliness and wild beauty. All day long they either "followed creeks," or wound around the sides of steep mountains, with sheer drop-offs below the narrow trail. Uncle Adam was no talker, but he was a skilled driver. Often it seemed that they must go over the edge, or that the mules could not climb the steps of rock up which they had to pull the heavy wagon; but always the danger was safely passed.

Isabel wished, however, that she had four hands instead of two, to hold on with.

Along the creeks, where the going, though very rough, seemed not so dangerous, they passed numbers of windowless log-houses, flanked by almost perpendicular corn-fields. Sometimes whole families—men, women, and children—were out hoeing corn; but Uncle Adam explained that the "crap" was about "laid by"; and more often crowds of children swarmed to the doors of the houses to see the wagon pass. Usually there was a withdrawing woman's face in the dark interior behind.

They met but few men during the day, and every one of these was riding, and carried a gun on arm or shoulder.

"Why do they all carry guns?" asked Isabel.

Uncle Adam considered a moment, then replied: "Hit's gen'ally squirrel-hunting time in Breathitt."

"Do you mean," she inquired, "that they all go armed on account of the 'war'?"

Uncle Adam's reply was to reach down in the wagon and remove some bundles of fodder from beneath his feet, exposing a Winchester rifle. "Best to be on the safe side," he whispered, dropping the fodder back.

The sun had set before they crossed the last mountain, White Doe; and it was almost dark and mist hung everywhere before they halted at Uncle Adam's house at the head of White Doe Creek, the halfway place.

A fat feather-bed with clean covers had never looked so good to Isabel; and she threw her weary body and racked bones across it, while Aunt Rhoda went into "t' other house" to put supper on the table. After eating, she fell into bed for good, never knowing when Aunt Rhoda and Uncle Adam got into the other bed in the room. Once in the night she was awakened by a terrific clap of thunder, and a heavy downpour of rain on the roof.

In the morning Uncle Adam appeared troubled. "Hit was a bad storm," he said, "and hit means tides, landslips, and quicks all along the way. Reason would say not go on; but the women might get tore-up in their minds about you, so I allow we'll ondertake hit."

Sure enough, the streams that had been low and clear yesterday were to-day yellow torrents. Often Isabel had to grab her suitcase and lift her feet up into the seat, as the water came swirling into the wagon-bed. The boxes of freight Uncle Adam was hauling to the women just had to take the water.

Isabel noticed that the Winchester no longer reposed on the wagon-floor, and asked the reason.

"We passed the county line when we crossed White Doe last night," Uncle Adam said. "Hit's only in Bloody Breathitt that a weepon is called for."

"They have no wars, then, in this county?"

"Oh, yes, they got one; but hit's more open and fa'r and squar—not laywaying and ambushing and sech, like in Breathitt, whar the wrong man gets kilt often as not. Life is tolable safe in this county, and talking hain't so dangerous, neither. I allus keep my mouth shet in Breathitt—have follered hit sence I were young. But here I can speak freer. Now this here war on Troublesome—"

"Oh, do you actually mean there is a war where Cousin Amy and the tents are?" cried Isabel, delightedly.

"Right thar at the Forks of Troublesome," replied Uncle Adam; "Fallons and Kents, they both live thar, and for nigh thirty year thar's been a sight of hate and bloodshed betwixt 'em. But they have fit in the open, and done their own killing, mostly—not hired hit done, like they foller doing in Breathitt; and so a man has more respects for 'em. Sence the two main heads, Fighting Fult Fallon and Red Rafe Kent, got kilt off things hain't been quite so bad. You see, Red Rafe he finally kilt Fighting Fult; and then young Fult you might say had a bound to revenge his paw, and he kilt Rafe; and then there was a spell of peace whilst young Fult was down at Frankfort a year—"

"Do you mean in the penitentiary?"

"Yes; and then whilst he fit a year in Cuby. But when he come home, 'peared like he was kindly wild-turned, and hit wa'n't no time till him and Rafe's boy, Darcy, started the war all over again. The two boys don't hardly ever meet without shooting, and they've wounded each other time and again, though not fatal; and t' other boys that runs with 'em has been kilt and wounded, and things is pretty bad.

But I heared tell that at a picnic the quare women give on the hill last Thursday, nigh all the county being thar, old Uncle Ephraim Kent, the grand-daddy of Troublesome, some way or 'nother persuaded Fult and Darcy to call a truce for the time the women stayed. I allow hit's true. But of course hit won't last—there's too long-lived a hate betwixt Kents and Fallons ever to raly die down."

He was interrupted by the stopping of the wagon, the bed of which had caught on a large boulder, hidden by the muddy water.

Without a word, or the least show of annoyance, Uncle Adam got out, waded the creek to the bank, climbed to a rail-fence not far away, and returned with a rail, with which, almost thigh-deep in water all the time, he prized and tugged till the wagon was detached from the rock.

Soon afterward they turned out of the creek, and up a mountain. When they were near the top, Uncle Adam, who was walking alongside, handed the lines to Isabel.

"Hold 'em a minute, sis, whilst I see what's on ahead."

He came back soon, saying, "Hit's a bad slip—the trail all kivered deep. I'll have to chop me a way out below."

Taking his axe, he plunged down the slope, chopping saplings and undergrowth as he went, and as far as possible avoiding big trees.

After quite a while he returned. "Get out, sis, if you feel to," he said; "but hit would be better if you stayed in and helt the lines, whilst I hang on to the wagon behind. The mules know how—jest hold 'em straight."

The slope was one of at least fifty degrees, and there was no ledge or bench anywhere below to break a possible descent of five or six hundred feet. Isabel's heart was in her mouth, but she let it come no farther. "All right," she said, between clenched teeth.

Straight down, therefore, the mules went, a cautious, crouching step at a time, holding the wagon back with their haunches and with Uncle Adam's help. It was a remarkable performance, as was also the sheer pull up again on the far side of the "slip."

"Looks skeerier than hit is," remarked Uncle Adam, when they were once again in the road, and the mules were resting and "blowing."

The next thing they hung on was a stump in the middle of the descending trail. "Never was kotched on that stump before," said Uncle

Adam; "the big rain has washed the road clean away on both sides. Good thing I fotched that-air rail along; I allowed I'd need hit a few times."

After more prizing, they again proceeded for quite a while without difficulty. Then, in a creek where numerous logs were floating, they undertook to "ride" one, and were held for a short time on its larger end.

The various mishaps took time, however, and when night fell they were still some miles from their destination, with rain again beginning.

"I'm purely afeared to risk Troublesome in the dark," said Uncle Adam. "Hit is well named—hit is full of quicks. We'll take the night here with Benjy Logan's folks, and go on to the Forks in the morning."

Controlling her disappointment as best she might, Isabel made friends with Benjy Logan's folks, slept with them, eight in a room, that night, and was treated with such kindness that she was almost reconciled to the delay.

Next morning the sky was clear, and their journey went well for an hour, until they turned into Troublesome Creek. Then, very soon, the wagon began to settle and sink, and the mules to strain in vain to pull it out.

"We've struck one," said Uncle Adam, calmly. "A man can't manage no way to shun all the quicks there is in this creek." He stepped out on the tongue and began ungearing the mules.

"I'll ride back yander to the last house we passed and get another team, and some men to help. You set right there on your feet and don't take no fear,—hit ain't aiming to settle much furder."

He rode back down the stream, and Isabel "sat on her feet" and watched the yellow "tide" hurry past her, and rise higher in the wagon-bed. Very soon, however, it seemed to reach its limit, and then she relaxed and abandoned herself to the spell of rushing water, green wooded slopes, and deep loneliness.

Her revery was broken by the plunging of a horse's hoofs in water, and the appearance of a horseman a short distance ahead. He rode straight down toward her, inquiring,—

"Did you strike a quick?"

"Yes," she said.

"You're the singer the women in the tents sont out for, hain't you?"

"Yes."

"I was sartain of hit. Where's Uncle Adam gone to?"

"To get another team and some help."

"He'll need hit," said the newcomer, surveying the wagon.

He was young and extremely handsome, with large dark eyes, blue-black hair, and olive skin, and he sat his horse with perfect grace. Though he did not remove his wide black hat in speaking to Isabel, his manner otherwise was courtesy itself.

"Hit'll take two teams every bit and grain of two hours to pull that wagon out," he said. "Better get up behind me and ride in."

"Thank you," she said, "but Uncle Adam might wonder what had become of me."

"That's a fact, too," he said. "Better wait till he gets back. I heared from the women you was on the way; and when the rain come up night before last, and again last night, I knowed there'd be tides, and you'd see trouble coming acrost. And this morning, knowing how mean the quicks is down Troublesome, I tuck a notion to ride down and see how things was."

"You are very kind," she said. "Although we've had rather a bad time, I've enjoyed every minute of it. You see, I love adventure, and something different, and I've certainly found it."

Her blue eyes shone, her hair blew about in golden-brown tendrils, her delicate skin was flushed.

"I'm proud you come in," he said, "and the women on the hill, they'll be proud, and everybody will, for now we can have a sight more singing and good times. Not that we hain't had 'em ever sence they come," he added.

"It must be very nice," she said.

"Hit beats anything ever was heared of. You see, the young folks in this country never seed no pleasure before, less'n hit was mean pleasure. We never knowed there was right pleasure. Them women don't fully sense what they're a-doing for us."

"I'm crazy to help them, and to see everything, and meet everybody. Life must be very interesting up here. I've read a lot, of course, about the feuds, and Uncle Adam tells me there is actually one right here on Troublesome Creek. Is that so?"

The young man flashed a searching glance into her face before replying, carelessly, "There has been some little trouble in past times."

"Do you know any of the people who carried it on?"

"Yes," he replied, indifferently.

"I do hope I shall meet them," she said; "it seems *so* romantic; just like living hundreds of years ago in *The Scottish Chiefs*, or some other old tale."

"War's bad, wherever you take hit," he remarked; "but sometimes hit's necessary. I seed something of hit down in Cuby year before last—though, of course, that was n't much of a fight."

"Oh, you were there, were you?"

"In what little there was. You live down in the Blue Grass, don't you?"

"Yes."

"Hit's a sight different from this country, hain't hit,—all so level and pretty and smoothed-looking. But lonesome."

"Oh, you've been there?"

"I passed through hit one time on my way to Frankfort."

"I don't see anything lonesome about it."

"Don't you? Well, any level land looks lonesome to me; hit's more friendly-like to see the hills mustering clost about, and not all drawed off flat and distant, like they keered nothing about nobody. While we wait for Uncle Adam," he suggested, "you might maybe feel to sing a song-ballat; I heared you was a fine singer, and I do love hit."

"All right," said Isabel. "What kind of songs do you like best?"

"Oh, something that kindly hurts my feelings."

Isabel cast about in her mind for something plaintive, hit upon "The Rosary," and sang it in her lovely, clear soprano.

"That hain't all?" he asked in surprise, when she stopped.

"Yes, that's all."

"I allowed hit was just taking a start," he said. "Hit leaves the true lovers parted, don't hit?"

"Yes."

"Well, I hain't got no use for hit, then," he said, decidedly. "The true lovers ought n't to be plumb parted, or kilt off, in the end. Don't you know nary 'nother?"

This time she tried "Oh, wert thou in the cauld blast," with its incomparable words and music.

"That's some better, though hit's too short, too," commented her hearer. "Don't you know no long ones, like we foller singing in this country?"

"I don't believe I do," she said. "Suppose you sing one yourself."

"No, I hain't no singer."

"Yes, I have a feeling that you are. I want to hear you."

"Well, anything to pass the time. I might try 'Turkish Lady.'"

He began a many-stanzaed ballad, having a robust tune with many queer, long-drawn notes—the story of an English lord who was captured by a Turkish one, and thrown into his deepest dungeon, to be released later by the Turk's lovely daughter, amid mutual vows of love and constancy. After "seven long years have rolled around," the Turkish lady "bundles up her finest clothing," and journeys to England, in search of her lagging lover. Arriving at his castle, and "tingling at the ring," she is informed by "the proud young porter" that his master is just bringing a new bride in. She gives him a message to take to his lord; and when he reports it, with the additional information,—

"There's the fairest lady standing yonder
That my two eyes did ever see;
She wears gold rings on every finger,
And on one finger she has three.
There's enough gay gold about her middle
To buy half of Northumberlee,"—

the master, recognizing his old true love from the description, under the stress of returning passion breaks his sword in pieces three, packs off the new bride with little ceremony, and celebrates another wedding with the Turkish lady, to the general admiration and glee.

Isabel listened, inexpressibly charmed. "Do you realize," she inquired, "that that ballad goes way back to the time of the Crusades, and is probably seven or eight hundred years old? Where did you learn it?"

"I never heared nothing of hits history," he said, "but hit's what I call a right ballat—hit turns out proper. My granny, she teached hit to me; she used to foller singing the night through on song-ballats."

"Oh, will you take me to see her?" asked Isabel.

"Sartain."

"And your voice is good, too; you'll be a great help to me in the singing classes."

Uncle Adam, another man, and the two teams came splashing up behind.

"I see you hain't been lonesome," remarked Uncle Adam.

"I allowed hit would be a bad time for you, getting acrost, and rid down to see how things was," explained the young man, with dignity. "I axed the singing woman to get up behind and ride in, but she said she felt to wait for you."

"Take her on along," said Uncle Adam. "We got to hitch the teams to the hind eend and pull out back'ards, if we do pull out, and hit'll be a couple hours at best, and I take hit she wants to see t'other women. Jump up behind, sis, and go in with him, and tell the women not to get out of heart, that I'm a-coming some time!"

The young man rode close alongside, took off his coat and spread it behind him, on the nag's back, and Isabel jumped from the wagon-seat and lit in the proper place. As she firmly grasped the hantle of the saddle, her fingers just grazed a pistol that protruded from her rescuer's pocket.

"Far'well till I come," called Uncle Adam, as they started up the creek. "Take keer of her, Fult!"

Isabel started violently at the name. Was it possible that the youth sitting before her on the saddle, in all his dashing beauty, was the young feud leader? He had certainly mentioned both Frankfort and Cuba. Thrilled through and through, and consumed with curiosity, she could not endure the suspense a moment longer.

"My name's Isabel Gwynne," she said. "What's yours?"

"Fult Fallon," he replied, gently touching the nag with his spur.

V

The Widow-Man

On the Thursday afternoon of the week following the quare women's Fourth-of-July picnic, a hollow-eyed, disheveled-looking man drew up before Uncle Lot Pridemore's gate, fell rather than dismounted from his mule, dropped his bridle over a paling, and stumbled into the yard and up on the porch.

Aunt Ailsie appeared from the rear of the house. "Jeems Craddock!" she exclaimed; "I had plumb give you out! But what ails you, Jeems? Here, set down, quick!"

She pushed a chair under him, and he slumped down in it on his backbone, long legs stretching across the porch, arms hanging lifelessly at his sides, chin dropped forward on his bosom.

Aunt Ailsie ran for a gourd of water. Jeems gulped it feebly.

"You look sick to death," she said, anxiously. "Maybe you better have something stronger."

She returned this time with a cup half full of a liquid that looked like water, but was much more eagerly drunk by Jeems.

"Eh law,—that's what I need; good corn-liquor, to holp me up a little."

"Hit's good, too," replied Aunt Ailsie; "hit's some Fulty fotched me t'other day; he allus keeps me in hit."

She waited for the corn-liquor to get in its work—until Jeems's chin was lifted from his breast, his hollow cheeks were flushed, his eyes had lost their dull stare.

"Now tell about hit, Jeems," she said, sympathetically.

He began in a weak voice, which gained strength as he proceeded.

"Ever since Mallie tuck 'n died in Aprile, hit's been the same old story—every night me up 'n down all night with the babe, a-fixing hits suck-bottle or a-walking hit for colic, and then getting up before day, maybe without ary wink of sleep, to cook breakfast, with likely the babe a-yelling all through, and t' other eight young-uns all a-squirming underfoot so bad hit makes me dizzy-headed. Then a-trying to get 'em all fed up, and them a-fighting and a-snatching all the time like wildcats, and not able to eat none myself for worriment and dyspepsy. Then a-starting the little gals on the dishes, and the oldest chaps on the firewood, whilst I go out to feed the property and milk the cow-brutes, and them cow-brutes so sot again' having a man-person come a-nigh 'em they do more devilment than all the young-uns. Then maybe, when I get back in, the babe has fell off the bed and nigh cracked hits head, and the young-uns is piled on the floor in a gineral fight, if they hain't sot the house afire playing with lightwood. And then I got to get 'em all onraveled again, and the fire put out, and the babe peaceified with a sugar-teat; and then sweep the main gorm of dirt out of the house, and spread the beds, whilst the chaps goes out again to dig 'taters and pick the beans for dinner. Which then I have to put 'em in the pot,—I give you my word, Aunt Ailsie, I hain't had time to string ary bean this summer,—and mix up a pone of bread and fix hit on the hairth where hit won't cook too hard. And all this before the day's work is raelly begun. And then hit's gether up every one of the nine,—babe, suck-bottle, and all, because I would n't dairst leave ary one behind,—and climb the hill to tend the crap; though there hain't but four of the young-uns, Miles and Joe and Minty and Phœbe, is nigh big enough to hold a hoe. T'other four has to take turns minding the babe, and not let hit fall off the hill or play with rattlesnakes. Then we work all morning, and when the sun-ball gets high, all hands comes down again to dinner, and then pull back up again and work till sundown, with the babe a-laying on a quilt between the rows, to take what naps of sleep hit gets, and t' others so drug-out and ill and feisty, they keep a-drapping their hoes and running off to hunt ground-hogs and 'possums, or quiling up somewheres and going to sleep too—and which I wisht they'd all sleep all the time, for then I'd see a little grain of peace. And then all down again to cook supper and feed the young-uns and t'other creeturs,—mules and hogs and chickens,—and milk them devilish cow-brutes again, and then get all hands off to bed, and me dead for a nap of sleep myself, but maybe not nary two hours hand-running all night long, what with the babe's manœuvres, and my dyspepsy—for no kind of food won't set on my stummick no more. And next day the whole thing all over again, if not wusser, with maybe washing or churning throwed in—and all the time the same old story—jest a hip-and-a-hurrah, and a rare-and-a-pitch, and a hoove-and-a-set, from one day's eend to t' other, till hit's the God's truth, Aunt Ailsie, I don't actually know whether I'm a-living in a turrible nightmare, or dead and gone to hell for my sins—and don't care, neither!"

Aunt Ailsie laid a compassionate hand on his arm. "Pore Jeems, pore creetur," she said; "things is wusser with you than I suspicioned, though I allowed they'd be bad enough when I heared Mallie was gone, and you with so many of a size, and nary one big enough to help. I've thought of you time and again, and wished I lived a-nigh you, so's I could do things for you. You allus was sech a good, diligent, working boy, the right son of your maw, that was my best friend when I was a young gal. Yes, I shore have pitied you in my heart; and that's the reason I sont you the word about these here fotched-on women; I allowed, in the bunch of 'em, you could find one to your notion, and pick you out a good wife. But that's neither here nor yander now; you air a sick man, Jeems, and not in no fix even to talk about courting; and what I aim to do is to put you to bed this minute."

"I would have started soon as the word come," groaned Jeems; "but first I had to lay the corn by; and then Jasper, one of the three-year-old twins, tuck a spell of the croup; and then Clevy, the five-year-old, chopped his big toe off, and Jemimy, the two-year one, was a-licking the milk out of the top aidge of the churn and went in head-foremost, and was black in the face and appeariently gone when we pult her out. And then seemed like I could n't no way on earth persuade nobody to come there and stay with them young-uns whilst I got away a couple of days—not nary neighbor would n't no way consent to hit; and I had to go clean yan side the mountain atter a widow-woman, Cindy Swope, with six of her own, that tuck pity-sake on me and come over, with the six, a-yesterday. And me so bad off by then I could n't hardly set my nag to get here."

"Pore Jeems—don't worry no more; you're here now, and in plenty of time, too; none of the quare women hain't stepped off yet. You get along there into t' other house, and shuck off, and lay down in the fur bed you laid in when you was here two year gone,—pore creetur, you look like a grandpaw now to the man you was then,—and I'll fetch you in a leetle hot snack that I'll gorrontee to set on your stummick, and then you'll take that nap of sleep you been dying for sence Aprile."

When Uncle Lot came in from work an hour later, snores were rising loudly and rhythmically from "t' other house." Aunt Ailsie simply said that Jeems Craddock, having a little business on Troublesome, had come to take the night; and, seeing he was sick, she had put him to bed at once—an explanation which satisfied Uncle Lot's stern but hospitable soul.

At supper Uncle Lot announced; "Atter studying on hit a week, careful, Ailsie, like I told you coming from the picnic I aimed to do, I have made up my mind to lend a cow to them women on the hill for the time they're here. We air commanded to remember the stranger that is within our gates, and hit appears like I feel to do that much for 'em, even if they have got a sight of wrong idees—sech as holding Sunday School for young-uns, when hit hain't once even spoke of in Scripter, and giving an overweight of larning to women-folks, and the like. And on that last line, too, I have been a studying, like I promised the women; and hit's true we air commanded to sarch the Scripters, and likewise that Paul says there hain't neither male nor female in Christ Jesus. Which, having clear Bible for, I am willing that you should larn jest enough from them women for you to be able to read Scripter, and no more, believing in my soul that larning in gineral is too much for a woman's mind."

"O paw, do you raelly mean you aim to let me get larning, same as Uncle Ephraim?" asked Aunt Ailsie, breathlessly.

"As fur as I told you," qualified Uncle Lot.

"Oh, praise the Lord!" exclaimed Aunt Ailsie. "O paw, I feel like I can't wait to take my first lesson! When can I start in?"

"I allow you can go in maybe a-Saturday," permitted Uncle Lot, graciously.

"And I'll drive the cow in then to the women, too. Which one do you want to lend 'em, paw, Old Pied, or the pieded heifer? Both has calves ready to wean, and both is milking fine—the heifer a leetle grain the best."

"Let 'em have her, then; I don't do nothing halfway. And there's five of them, and not but two of us."

But Aunt Ailsie did not have to take the cow in herself. Next morning, which was Friday, Fult dashed up the branch.

"I'm on my way down Troublesome a piece," he called, "and allowed I'd ride up and just say how-d'ye, and see how you was."

Aunt Ailsie ran down to the fence. "S-sh—don't talk so loud; there's a sick man a-laying in there asleep," she said. "I'm proud you come, for your grandpaw has tuck a notion to lend them quare women a cow, and you can drive her back with you. And, another thing, Fulty, he has studied on hit and made up his mind to let me get larning,—enough to read Scripter, anyway,—and which I'm a-coming in to-morrow to take my first lesson!"

"I'm glad for you, granny," said Fult, heartily, "and I'd take the cow right back, now, but I'm on my way to see what has happened to the singer the women sont out for, that ought to have got in last night. But the rains have been so bad I allow traveling is pore, and Uncle Adam's wagon is maybe stalled in a quick down Troublesome, and I told the women I'd ride down a piece and see. But I'll come for the cow later in the day—soon as dinner's over, maybe."

Returning to the house, Aunt Ailsie tiptoed into the room where Jeems slept, and came out with a large armful of his clothes over her arm. These she threw on a chair in the kitchen-house, then held up the coat and trousers, with a deep sigh.

"Hain't hit a pyuore pity, now, for a man-person to start out a-courting in sech gear?" she exclaimed. "Pore creetur, the babe has puked up hits milk all over him from head to foot, and the dust has got kotched in the spots, till nobody would n't be able to tell the color of his coat and breeches. And them fine linsey, too, that Mallie weaved herself out of black sheep's wool for him."

She went to work with hot water and soft soap, repeatedly sousing the coat and trousers and socks, and rubbing them with her hands (wash-boards were an unknown luxury). Then, having cleansed and rinsed them, she hung them out in the July sun to dry, and turned her attention to the hat, which was the usual broad-brimmed black felt of the mountain man.

"Eh law, hain't hit a picter of misery!" she said, holding it out: "the brim all a-flopping, like hits ambition was plumb gone."

She scrubbed and cleaned it, and then took a flatiron and pressed the brim carefully while it was still damp, until it took on quite a jaunty stiffness.

Then came the shoes. The deeply caked mud was scraped and washed off, and a mixture of lard and soot generously applied.

By ten o'clock the suit was sufficiently dry to be pressed, and a truly artistic job was made of it.

Then Aunt Ailsie went in and waked Jeems. "You've put in seventeen hours good sleep," she said, "and I allow your stummick needs a leetle comfort next. You got plenty of time to get ready for dinner. I fotched you in a pan of warm water and soap and a towel and washrag, allowing you might feel to take a good wash-off. Then you can put on this here clean shirt of Lot's,—I could n't get yourn off'n you to wash hit,—and these here breeches I washed for you, and clean socks and shoes, and then come in the kitchen-house and take you a shave with Lot's strop and razor, and then I'll crap your hair,—hit looks like hit hain't seed scissors sence Mallie died,—and then you'll begin to feel more like yourself."

An hour later, Jeems, washed, dressed, shaved, shingled, and combed, was indeed a transformed man—the hollow look gone from eyes and cheeks, twenty years from his age.

"If you could meet up with yourself, Jeems, you would n't never know hit was the same man rid up here a-yesterday," said Aunt Ailsie, proud of her handiwork. "You look now about what you air— thirty-two come September; I ricollect your birth, you and Link being nigh of an age. You look fitten now to start out a-courting to-morrow. Not," she added hastily, seeing an awakening gleam in Jeems's eye, "not to court young gals, of course, but to court them of an age with you. Of course, you'll never be what you once was, in those fur-off young days when me 'n' your maw used to take pride in your looks."

"Hit seems to me like two or three weeks sence yesterday," remarked Jeems, who appeared to be in a kind of daze. "I don't noways feel like the same man."

"You hain't," pronounced Aunt Ailsie. "You was in a pure franzy for sleep. And now you got hit, hit has wropt up your narves, and swaged down your feelings, and knit up your faculties, till you're in some fix to look around you and get things kindly straightened out in your mind, and take counsel about what you come for—the job of getting you a wife.

"Now I knowed in reason you'd be a-seeing troubles, though I never tuck the full measure of 'em, or drempt how nigh crazed and drove you was. But when these here furrin women come in, and I seed how smart and pretty they was, and all the way from twenty-three to twenty-eight year old, and nary a man to their name, seemed like hit went through me like a knife, I felt so bad for sech sweet creeturs to be old maids. And then I thought right off of you, and how scand'lous bad you needed a wife, and your young-uns a maw, and how proud you'd be doing yourself to get one of these fine, fotched-on women; and I jest put two and two together, Jeems, and sont you word immediate, afore any more widow-men could get in ahead of you; for you know they's allus several round about, all on the look, and I knowed when they seed these women they'd be atter 'em hot-foot. And when you did n't come sooner, I begun to get right scared for your chances. But I hope you hain't too late yet.

"Now, Jeems, hit's plain enough you can't live no longer a widder—you'll sartain be dead if you do. And the pint is, what kind of a woman do you need? That's what you want to study on, and study keerful. You hain't had no show sence Mallie died, to get out and look around none, or do much thinking either, I allow. But hit don't take much studying to know you need, first and fore-most, a woman that can tame down and civilize young-uns."

"That's hit," Jeems agreed, fervently.

"All them furrin' women knows how to handle young-uns to the queen's taste," continued Aunt Ailsie. "You'd never believe how civil all them feisty, briggaty boys and gals at The Forks has got to be."

"Hit's a sight how a woman-person can swage 'em down," said Jeems, wonderingly. "Now, Cindy Swope had n't been in the house a hour afore she had my nine and her six all a-working peaceable and biddable."

"And the next thing you want, Jeems, with your dyspepsy, and all that mess of young-uns, is somebody can cook good."

"Eh, law, that's what I want, too! I'm plumb beat out with my own cooking; that air supper Cindy cooked when she come in was the first meal of vittles had sot on my stummick for three month.'"

"I don't rightly know," continued Aunt Ailsie, "which one of them quare women is the best cook, but, from the table they set, I allow they all air. Now there's one that's sort of extry fine on vittles and larns the gals how to make all manner of new-fangled things, and hain't but twenty-three, and got mighty pretty crow's-wing hair, and blue eyes. But ricollect, she hain't for you, Jeems, and would n't so much as look at a old widow-man with nine young-uns. And, anyhow, Darcy Kent's a-talking to her. So don't you waste no thoughts there.

"And the next thing you got a bound to have is a woman can sew and weave and spin, same as Mallie, and keep coats and blankets for you and your young-uns. Now one of them head-women—Amy is her name—is the sewingest woman ever I seed, besides the ladyest; why, she's even got Fulty and his wild crowd of boys a-hemming handkerchers and towels up yander every day, and she has already axed me to larn her how to weave and spin. She'd be the woman for you, Jeems, if you could get her—either her, or t' other head one, Virginny, which is the up-and-comingest female ever I laid an eye on, and don't baulk at nothing on earth. And then, of course, the nurse-woman, she'd be mighty handy when the young-uns all takes down sick with the choking disease, or the breast-complaint, or sech; or likewise that one that teaches the least ones, and keeps about fifty of 'em happy and biddable all the time. You could n't make no mistake, whichever of them four you tuck, Jeems."

Jeems meditated a moment, then said, with a deep groan: "One thing you left out, Aunt Ailsie, and seems like hit's the one I set the most store by of all. I want me a woman knows how to milk good, and handle cow-brutes. Hit appears like I could have stood up under all the rest, but for them devils of cow-brutes on my hands, that gets mad whenever I come a-nigh 'em, just because I am a man-person, and upsets the bucket, and holds up their milk, and kicks me in the shins, and does their almightiest to aggravate and destroy me, till my gorge rises up at the very thoughts of 'em. Yes, Aunt Ailsie, I want me a woman can milk, if she can't do nothing else. Now, Cindy, hit was a sight—."

"Sartain you do, Jeems," interrupted Aunt Ailsie; "but there hain't no needcessity in the world to bother about that. *Any* woman anywheres can milk,—hit's woman's *nature* to,—and I allow every single one of them fotched-on women is the finest milkers ever was; they so smart any way you take 'em.

"But listen, Jeems,"—and there was a sudden, inspired gleam in her eye,—"if that's what you set the most store by, me 'n' Lot is a-lending a cow to them women this very day,—the pieded heifer,—and Fulty is a-coming to drive her in atter dinner. And I never allowed to let you go in where them women was till you had got you another night of sleep. But sarcumstances changes plans, and I don't know but what hit might be better for you to go in with Fulty this evening, unbeknownst to the women, and kindly take a gineral view, and spy out the land, so to speak, and see for yourself who is the ablest milker; and then come back and sleep on hit to-night; and then to-morrow you and me will go in and take the day,—I was a-going in anyhow to start on my A B C's,—and I'll fix a way so's you'll get a chanct to court the one you pick out—I allus was the most contrivingest woman you ever seed. And if all goes well, as hit sartainly will, you'll ride home a-Sunday with your wife behind you, and likewise all your troubles and trials."

Jeems agreed that the plan was a good one; indeed, he began to wake up and be quite keen on the scent; so much so that Aunt Ailsie felt impelled to drop a few more words of wisdom.

"Of course, I know a man's nature, and in partic'lar a widow-man's, is to run atter the youngest and foolishest female that crosses his trail, with nary thought for his orphant offsprings, or his own welfare. But take the counsel of one that has lived long and seed much and thinks a sight of you, Jeems, and pick you out a good, old, settled woman, nigh of an age with you, that's got more, or anyway as much, on the inside of her headpiece as the outside, and will be a right step-maw and help-meet. Twenty-eight is terrible old, I know, most women being nigh-grandmaws by then; but I give you my hand, Jeems, them two head-women, Amy and Virginny, is the deceivingest in their looks ever you seed, and don't ary one of 'em look hardly twenty; hit's a pure myxtery how old women like them can keep sech a fair, tender skin, and rosy jaws, and shiny hair, and white teeth.

"And another thing for you to bear in mind constant, Jeems, is that no young gal, with a-plenty of chances ahead of her, would n't take a second look at a old widow-man with nine orphant young-uns. No, a woman would have to be pretty far along on the cull-list before she'd even think of tying up with a man in your condition. Facts is facts, Jeems, and ought to be looked full in the eye."

Uncle Lot stepped in just then, and the subject was, of necessity, dropped. Jeems ate a ravenous dinner, and with every bite courage and manhood seemed to grow within him.

Not long after dinner, Fult appeared, as he had promised. Aunt Ailsie went to the pasture-bars with him to get the pieded heifer. Seeing an unwonted light in his handsome eyes, she inquired: "What's come to you, Fulty—what's happened?"

"Oh, nothing," replied Fult, carelessly. "I found that air singer this morning, down Troublesome, setting in Uncle Adam's wagon, stalled in a quick, and brung her up behind me to the women."

"Is she an old maid, too?"

"No," answered Fult, indignantly.

"How old is she?"

"I never axed her; but she looks about sixteen."

"Is she a pretty looker?"

"Prettiest you ever seed," declared Fult with feeling.

"Prettier than Lethie?"

Fult flushed. "She's different," he said. "And sing! I never in life heared the like?"

"I'll be bound she can't outsing me when I were young," said Aunt Ailsie, jealously.

"Maybe not," replied Fult; "I never heared you then. I told her about you, and she wants to hear you."

When Fult and Jeems were mounted, and ready to start with the heifer, Aunt Ailsie gazed with pride upon her handiwork. Jeems made quite a presentable appearance. True, a collar and tie would have improved the effect; but such vanities were only for dashing young blades like Fult, not for old, settled, married- or widow-men.

After they had started, Aunt Ailsie called Jeems back for a last anxious word.

"Mind now," she said, "not to get your thoughts tangled up with no young gals you may see there. One's jest come in this morning from the level land. Ricollect, they hain't for sech as you. Keep your mind fixed stiddy on what you're a-going atter, and don't get witched off by no young face with naught behind hit."

When they arrived at the tents, the heifer was received with warm appreciation by two of the women, whom Jeems judged to be the heads, though they were astonishingly fair and rosy and young and neatly dressed, to have reached the ancient age of twenty-eight. From a safe distance in the background, Jeems inspected each, narrowly and appraisingly. When the heifer had been anchored to a tree, one of the women returned to a group of old people she appeared to be teaching, near by, and the other settled down to letter-writing under a more distant tree. Fult had hurried up-hill, and Jeems slowly followed, gazing with solemn, owlish eyes upon all the strange things and people he saw.

The lowest tents were deserted, but in the larger, gayly decorated one farther up, two or three dozen mothers, with babies, were gathered, and the nurse was giving a talk on the care of infants, using one in her demonstration. She was giving it a warm bath when Jeems peered into the tent. He was at once transfixed.

"That air woman knows how to handle a young-un," he said to himself, after watching the proceedings for some time, "and is a good looker, too."

No mother present could have been more appreciative of the deft ways of the nurse than was Jeems, out of the fullness of his own experience.

After this was over, he went on to the top of the spur, where the young folks of different ages were gathered, in several large groups and circles, playing games. In the largest circle, where the young men and maidens were playing "Old Bald Eagle," a game that was a combination of quadrille and Virginia reel, with a song accompaniment,

Fult was leading, and his partner was a young and extremely pretty stranger, at the sight of whom Jeems stopped stone-still and gazed with all his eyes. Aunt Ailsie's warning came to him with a pang after a while: "Ricollect, sech as that hain't for you." He sighed deeply, and felt a dull anger with Fult's youth and beauty.

Still another very young and pretty one—the one with the "crow's-wing hair and blue eyes"—sat on a bench not far away; but Darcy Kent was at her side.

After a long while, the play-games stopped, and the merry crowd trooped down the hill and home—all save Fult and a few of his cronies, who stopped at the big tent, where Fult was soon picking a banjo and singing ballads for the stranger. Jeems leaned against a tree-trunk outside, and waited for the fateful hour of milking to arrive.

Finally, an anxious call came from below for Fult, and all in the tent went down, Jeems following at a little distance. Fult joined the group of women behind the cooking-tent. When Jeems arrived, he saw that they were gathered anxiously about the heifer. One of them, Virginia, was saying to Fult:—

"But how are we going to get her milked?"

Fult shook his head. "I allowed, and granny allowed, all you women could milk—all the women-folks in this country can."

"Milk? Why, I never did such a thing in my life! Down in the Blue Grass the women don't milk; the men do all the heavy work like that."

Jeems stopped in his tracks. His jaw dropped.

"I thought maybe you could milk her for us to-night, and until we could hire somebody for the job," continued Virginia, a little impatiently.

Fult flushed. "Sorry I can't oblige you," he said; "I never in life undertook to milk a cow. Up in this country hit's allus a woman's job."

"Do you mean to say you let your mother and sisters do rough work like milking all the time?"

Fult laughed. "Maw would n't let me get in ten foot of her cow," he said. "Cows won't stand for hit in this country. They are used to women-folks and their ways, and don't want a man to come a-nigh 'em."

"Hit's a fact," groaned Jeems inwardly, from the depths of experience.

"You women know there hain't nothing I would n't do to pleasure you," continued Fult, gallantly. "If I knowed how to milk, I'd try hit, man's job or not. But a body can't learn all in a minute."

"They can't, neither," protested Jeems, under his breath.

"Can't a single one of you brought-on women milk a cow?" inquired Fult, looking in astonishment around the circle.

One after another, Amy, the nurse, the kinder-gartner, the cooking teacher, the singing gal, admitted her ignorance. None had ever in her life tried to milk.

Jeems's jaw was now permanently dropped, his eyes stared with amazed incredulity.

"And even if some of them could milk," said Virginia, with a note of decision in her soft voice, "I should n't feel that I could permit them to do it. It's setting too bad an example. The thought of the women of this country doing all the milking shocks me inexpressibly, and one of the principal things I hope to teach them is that milking is *not* a woman's job, and should be done always and entirely by the men."

Jeems's countenance registered complete horror.

At this instant, Isabel, the new arrival, spoke up. "The cow will have to be milked to-night by somebody," she said; "and though I never milked in my life, and do not approve of women milking, still I'd be glad to try this time, if you say so, Cousin Amy, and Miss Virginia. Of course, I live on a stock-farm,—papa has always raised thoroughbred horses and cattle,—and I've seen cows milked by the negro men thousands of times, and it does seem that I ought to be able to do it myself. If you'll give me a bucket, I'll be glad to try."

Virginia shook her head. "I don't consider it wise," she said; "it's setting too bad a precedent."

"I believe I'd let her do it just this once, as it's an emergency," suggested Amy, in her quiet way.

"Well, maybe for just this once," Virginia grudgingly consented.

A shining bucket was produced, and Isabel stepped toward the heifer. Jeems's face was once more transformed, irradiated.

"Now you hold her," said Isabel to Fult. "Not that I'm a bit afraid. I can ride any horse I ever saw; but I'm not so used to cows."

She approached carefully, spoke to the heifer, rubbed down her flank, and at last gently grasped a teat. This she squeezed periodically and persistently for a long while. Not a drop of milk appeared.

"Why, there's something the matter with this cow," she said at last. "I believe she's a dry one."

"No, granny said she was giving three straight gallons a day right along," said Fult; "and to not fail to milk her a single time."

Isabel tried another teat, then conscientiously made the rounds of all.

"Maybe she's just too excited to have any milk to-day," said Virginia. "I've heard that cows are extremely nervous creatures."

"Yes, that must be it," said Isabel. At last she rose, reluctant to give up, but forced to admit that she could do nothing.

Jeems's expression was now one of utter be-wilderment. But he was ready to accept the explanation offered—a cow-brute was equal to anything.

A small boy of eleven or twelve, who had been standing near all the time, digging his toes into the earth, spoke up laconically.

"Anybody with eyes could see she's got milk."

"Well, how can you tell, Billy?" asked Virginia.

"Because I know cows. I've holp maw milk a many of a time, and Lethie, too. I don't care if hit hain't a man's job, I've holp 'em when they was sick or busy. Here, you fotched-on women don't know nothing; gimme that air bucket, and a apern and sunbonnet, and I'll show you. Of course, she would n't lemme come a-nigh her in breeches."

The nurse lent her large apron, Amy her white sunbonnet, and Billy, retiring to the cooking-tent to put them on, soon emerged, hit the cow a sharp lick on the hip, bawled "Saw!" half a dozen times, squatted down, put out small dirty hands, and in an instant two large jets of milk were foaming into the pail.

"I knowed hit," commented Billy, scornfully; "I got my opinion of a passel of women that hain't able to milk a cow betwixt 'em!"

The women looked on in solemn relief.

And Jeems? He swept the six strange women with a slow glance, in which indignation, disgust, and anguish struggled for supremacy; then, turning on his heel, strode rapidly down the hill.

"Not nary one of 'em able to milk a cow!" he exclaimed to himself over and over, as he descended; and later, as he rode down Troublesome: "Not nary single one! Not even," with a groan, "that air youngest and prettiest!"

It was supper-time when he arrived, and Uncle Lot being present, there was no chance for Aunt Ailsie to ask the reason of his profound melancholy, which, however, was so noticeable that, when she started to milk after supper, she called to him to go with her.

"What in creation's the matter with you, Jeems?" she demanded. "You look like you had seed a hant!"

"I've seed worse'n a hant, Aunt Ailsie," he said, with awful solemnity: "I've seed six able-bodied women, not nary one of which is able to milk a cow-brute!"

Aunt Ailsie dropped her bucket. "Jeems!" she said, "you know hit hain't the truth!"

"Hit's the truth, too," he replied, sternly. "When milking-time come, not nary one of 'em would even try but one,—that air newest and youngest,—and she could n't squeeze out a drap! And then a leetle chap that was hanging around, he sot down and milked out a bucketful easy as scat!"

Aunt Ailsie picked the bucket up, and stood by the bars, speechless.

"I never once thought but what every woman on that hill was a able milker," she said at last. "But look-a-here, Jeems, all hope hain't yet gone; they would any or all larn to milk if needcessity come—say if any of 'em was to marry a widow-man!"

Jeems shook his head most emphatically. "They would n't, neither," he said. "Them women all allowed hit was a man's job, not a woman's, to milk a cow-brute; and one of them head-women said she was aiming to teach all the Women-folks in this here country not to milk nary 'nother time theirselves, but to make the men-folks do hit allus."

Jeems's voice broke on the utterance of this frightful heresy, and Aunt Ailsie herself was entirely beyond speech.

After a long while she recovered herself, and laid down the bars. "Well, hit jest wa'n't to be, Jeems," she said; "hit just wa'n't predestyned for you to get you a fotched-on woman. I don't know but what, if I was you, I'd court that air widow-woman, Cindy Swope. Her six and your nine, with maybe seven or eight more to foller, will be kindly a stumbling-block; but if she can quell both young-uns and cow-brutes, like you say, numbers won't make no p'ticlar difference—you'll still have peace in your home. I reckon hit's the best all round, Jeems; though I feel mighty onreconciled, atter all the big plans I laid for you. You hain't the first man to look furder and fare worse."

She threw half a dozen nubbins to Old Pied, sat down on the small three-legged stool, and began to milk, vigorously but pensively.

Jeems gazed down upon her, with healing and comfort stealing over every torn and jangled nerve.

"Man's job, indeed!" he said to himself, scornfully; "Cindy hain't got no sech crazy notions!"

VI

Devil's Ditties

THE day following the widow-man's disastrous visit to the women on the hill, Aunt Ailsie came in, as she had planned, to get her first taste of learning. She had also planned, of course, to bring Jeems in and engineer his courting; and her disappointment was keen as she rode along on old Darb, meditating pensively upon the tragedy of the day before.

"They throwed away as good a chanct as ary old maid could look to have, and all because not a single one of 'em was able to milk a cow. I'm clean out of heart, and hain't aiming to trouble my mind to hunt up nary 'nother husband for 'em. Hit would n't be no use if I did, there not being a living man in this country would marry a woman that can't milk. May be that's the reason they hain't kotched 'em a man down in the level land."

Before Aunt Ailsie reached the tents on the hill, she saw her "pieded" heifer picking around up near the timber line, and sighed deeply.

"Pore creetur, I'd never a-lent you to 'em if I had knowed; hit'll be your ruination having that air little Billy Lee feisting round you."

When she reached the tents, the cooking class was over, as was also the sewing lesson, and the singing was just beginning in the largest tent, where even more young folks than usual were gathered.

Amy was playing the baby organ, but Virginia, who stood near her, straightening up the book-shelves, saw Aunt Ailsie and beckoned for her. As she approached the two, she sighed deeply again.

"Pore gals, they don't know what they missed yesterday; they don't know how nigh they come to being tuck off the cull-list!"

Her attention was immediately drawn from them to the newcomer of whom Fult had spoken the day before—a lovely young girl who led the singing, and sang as spontaneously and joyously as a mocking-bird, and whose example was contagious, for the more timid young people, who had sung haltingly before, now poured their whole souls into the delight of it. Fult's voice was the best among the young men, and blended well with that of the new singer.

Aunt Ailsie sat down on a bench and listened, somewhat critically, for half an hour. "Fulty was right," she said to herself then, "she can outsing me when I was a young gal. But I misdoubt if she knows as many song-ballats as I knowed."

There was so much enthusiasm that the usual half-hour of singing lengthened into an hour, and was ended only by the ringing of the dinner-bell below.

"We're so glad you came," said Amy, as the two started down the hill; "we want to tell you how very grateful we are for the cow."

"Yes," said Virginia, joining them; "nothing could be a greater blessing to us."

"I heared not nary one of you was able to milk her," said Aunt Ailsie; and she could not keep all reproach out of her voice.

"No, but Billy Lee can, and we've hired him to do it regularly, and the milk is delicious, and we've bought us a churn this morning."

"She's a right cow," said Aunt Ailsie; "but"—solemnly—"hit takes a woman-person to get the best out of a cow." She sighed deeply. "But, women, that's neither here nor yander now; what I come for to-day was to tell you my man has give his consent for me to get larning — enough, anyhow, to read Scripter, though no more."

"Oh, we're so glad for you—you must have your first lesson right after dinner."

"That's what I aim to; 'pears like I can't hardly wait to begin."

Just then Fult came up behind and laid a detaining hand on Aunt Ailsie's arm. "Stop a minute, granny—here's somebody craves to meet you."

Aunt Ailsie fell back behind the others. "Oh, the singing gal!" she exclaimed, looking for a long minute into Isabel's face, then turning her around for a rear view, and summing up the inventory with "Now, hain't she pretty as a poppet!"

Fult's eyes expressed concurrence.

"What's your name, daughtie?"

"Isabel Gwynne."

"How old air you?"

"Twenty."

"You don't look hit. You hain't got ary man yet, I allow?"

"No."

"Well, praise the Lord there's one amongst the quare women hain't a old maid! You got a whole year to go on yet, and, judging by your looks, you'll likely land a man before hit's over. I heared you sing this morning, and hit was fine. I follered singing myself when I were young."

"Yes, Mr. Fallon told me about it; he said you used to be able to sing ballads the night through, and never repeat yourself."

"Eh law, yes."

"And that you taught him those he knows. He has sung two or three for me, and I'm crazy about them, and can hardly wait to hear more. I hoped maybe you might sing for me this afternoon."

Aunt Ailsie drew back, with a frightened expression. "My fathers!" she said; "hit would be as much as my life is worth to sing song-ballats in public this way; my man can't abide 'em sence he j'ined; he allows they are devil's ditties, and won't have one raised under his roof."

"But this is n't his roof," laughed Isabel, glancing up at the sky.

"Eh law, when Lot says roof, he means anybody belongs under his roof. If I was to sing on this here hill, the news would travel over the county in less time than hit takes to tell hit, and Lot would be everly scandalized amongst the Old Primitives, and the sky would nigh fall. Now, though I hain't the songster I used to be, I *feel* to sing for you. I love hit better'n life, seems like. But a woman don't dairst to fly right pine-blank in the face of Scripter and disobey her husband!"

"No, I suppose not," admitted Isabel; "but how did you teach Mr. Fallon?"

Aunt Ailsie leaned forward and spoke in Isabel's ear. "I done hit unbeknownst!" she said: "I tuck Fulty up on top the ridge, and a leetle yan side, where no human could n't hear, and my man could n't noway be scandalized!"

"Well, why not take me up sometime, too?"

Aunt Ailsie gazed at the singing gal with dilating eyes. "I'll do hit, I shorely will," she declared. Then she continued, in a conspirator's voice: "We'll have to bide our time till Lot goes to a far funeral occasion, and can't get back afore night. Funeral meetings is setting in, now the crap's laid by; I heared Lot say several was denounced a-Sunday at a nigh one he went to. He'd ruther die as to miss one,—funeral meetings is his delight, same as song-ballats is mine,—and I'll listen round and find out when a far one is aiming to be, and get the word to Fulty, and Fulty can fetch you down to take the day, and then we'll have a singing time, up on the ridge."

Fult and Isabel entered joyfully into the conspiracy, and then all three went down, Isabel and Aunt Ailsie to the women's dinner-table, Fult to the hotel below.

After dinner, Aunt Ailsie received from Amy a brand-new primer, with her name written large on the front page, and thereupon attacked the alphabet with trembling enthusiasm, and the remark, "I feel like I'm jest starting in to live."

Soon afterward, several other old people came up the hill with their primers, and Amy heard them all recite the alphabet, and spell a number of words. Uncle Ephraim could even read a few sentences—evidently he was giving all his time and strength to the acquisition of knowledge.

He congratulated Aunt Ailsie on her start. "Hit's the best day's work you ever done," he said; "I would n't take the riches of the world for what I have larned these two weeks."

Later, Aunt Ailsie went up to see the play-games of the young folks on the spur. In the largest ring she saw Fult leading the song and play, with Isabel as his partner. Lethie, who had led with him hitherto, sat near by on a log, with little Madison, her baby brother, in her lap. Aunt Ailsie dropped down beside her.

"How's all the young-uns, Lethie?" she inquired.

"Oh, fine," replied Lethie; "that nurse woman, she cyored up the rash little Maddy was broke out with so bad; and t' others is seeing the time of their lives a-larning and playing on the hill, and don't never give me ary grain of trouble."

"Why hain't you playing yourself to-day?"

"I just did n't feel like hit."

"But that hain't right, Lethie; you air young, and ought to take your pleasure. Hit hain't right for a young gal to get old afore her time."

Lethie's under lip trembled a little. "Aunt Ailsie," she said, "the reason I hain't a-playing is, my clothes looks so quare."

She looked down at her dark, heavy linsey skirt, coarse little shoes, and ill-fitting pink-calico waist.

"What's the matter with 'em?" inquired Aunt Ailsie.

"I don't know; I allowed they was all right till yesterday. But sence Miss Isabel come in, they look so quare, and I hain't aiming to shame Fulty by playing with him. He axed me, but I would n't."

Aunt Ailsie scrutinized Isabel's simple white linen dress.

"Why, she hain't dressed no finer than you," she said.

"No, but she's different—her clothes sets so good on her. I think she's the prettiest woman ever I seed."

Aunt Ailsie looked at the lovely, wistful little face turned up to hers—the skin of milky whiteness, the big, heavily lashed gray eyes, the brave little mouth, the mass of pale golden hair drawn tightly back from forehead and temples, and twisted in a hard knot at the back.

"I don't see as she's any ahead of you on looks," she decided.

"Oh, I never did have no *looks*," said Lethie, deprecatingly; "but," earnestly, "I wisht I did have some clothes!"

"Pore child, you hain't got ary grain of chance to be young and gayly, like you ought, with your maw dead and gone, and your paw's house and all that mess of young-uns on your hands. Hit's a pure shame for a young gal to be burdened down that way."

"Oh, no, Aunt Ailsie," cried Lethie, in warm protest; "hit is my heart's delight to do for the young-uns sence maw died; I love them so good, and they love me so good, and little Maddy here is the sweetest babe ever was borned, and I can't stand to have him out of my sight."

Aunt Ailsie shook her head. "Hit hain't right," she insisted; "your paw ought to get him a good woman, that would treat the young-uns kind, and give you a chance to be young and happy."

"But I'm happy now," declared Lethie; "seems like I hain't had nothing but happiness sence these women come in—just all manner of good times. And paw says I am larning to cook so fine; and Charlie hain't been drunk nary time sence the Fourth of July, and Fulty behaving so civil—why, hit seems very near like heaven, and I just love all them women to death for coming, and this here new one most of all, because she's the smilingest and prettiest."

"You're a mighty good little gal; the Lord'll bless you for hit!"

Here the game broke up, and Fult came over to get Lethie for the next one.

"You go right on now, and don't be so back'ard," insisted Aunt Ailsie. "I'll tend the least one for you."

At her urging, Lethie went. But Isabel was playing just opposite, with Charlie as her partner; and every minute Lethie realized how much longer her own skirt was in the back than in the front, how clumsy her shoes were, how much too big and baggy her waist, and before long she said to Fult: "I hain't feeling good; you'll have to get you another pardner,"—and slipped out of the ring, shortly afterward going down the hill, with little Madison in arms, as Aunt Ailsie went.

Next morning, when Fult came across the street as usual to take her to the women's Sunday School, Lethie made an excuse not to go; and, after starting off all the children but little Madison, she went downstairs into her father's store and hunted among the shelves for some white goods like Isabel's dress. But, though there were several bolts of calicoes and ginghams, there was nothing in the way of white stuff save a piece of "bleached factory" (white domestic). From this she cut enough for a dress for herself and one for little Madison; then, hastening back upstairs, went to work with awkward little hands to try to cut and fit them, attempting to make her own as much like Isabel's as possible.

Every morning of the week following she went up the hill with Charlotta and Ruby Fallon, to the cooking classes, her little brother always on her arm; but she did not go to the play-parties in the afternoons, keeping this precious time and privacy for work on her white dress and Madison's. Saturday she finished both, the result, so far as her own was concerned, being pathetic; and Sunday she dressed herself and the baby in them, and waited for Fult to come for her again.

Instead, however, she was a little shocked to see him riding down Troublesome, with Isabel on a nag beside him.

She did not feel at all hurt or angry—in her eyes Fult was perfect; what he did must be all right. Gulping down a few tears, she hugged and kissed little Madison, took off her finery and his, and went to work doing some extra cooking for dinner.

Fult and Isabel were riding down to Aunt Ailsie's to hear the devil's ditties, Uncle Lot having gone to a funeral meeting fourteen miles away. It was the first time they had been alone together since the day Fult had brought Isabel in behind him. Meanwhile, she had heard fully about the "war" and Fult's part in it, had seen him play in the same game with his archenemy, Darcy Kent, had watched both impassive faces with fascinated eyes, and had developed a consuming curiosity to know just how feudists feel on the inside.

They had ridden only a short distance past the village when Isabel said, suddenly: "Why did n't you tell me that day you brought me in that you were one of the leaders of the 'war'?"

Fult started, flushed slightly, and replied: "I allowed you'd hear hit soon enough anyhow."

"But you knew how excited I was to hear from Uncle Adam that there was a feud right here on Troublesome. Of course, I had heard and read of them all my life,—my father had always taken a special interest in them—but to walk right into one as I did seemed too wonderful for words."

"But you walked into perfect peace," smiled Fult.

"Oh, yes, I know—the truce," said Isabel. "But that's just a temporary thing, is n't it? Just for the summer?"

"Yes."

"And then?"

Fult paused a moment before answering, deliberately: "I allow one or t' other of us will have to die before there's any lasting peace."

"Oh, why?" exclaimed Isabel; "why keep up the enmity and hatred? Why not let it die out forever?"

Fult was gazing straight ahead with drawn brows at a spot in the road.

"It hain't possible," he said, in a low voice. "But I can't talk about hit—never could, not even to my best friend, Charlie Lee. The onliest way is for me to keep hit all pinned right down inside me."

Suddenly he put out a hand, seized Isabel's bridle, and turned both the nags sharply aside into the creek.

"Right there, in the road," he said, in a choked voice, "is where they kilt my paw—come on him unexpected from them spruce-pines. I allus turn out of the road here."

"Oh, horrible!" exclaimed Isabel. "Oh, what you must have suffered! Can you forgive me for speaking lightly as I did about the war? For speaking of it at all? I can hardly forgive myself!"

Her blue eyes gazed insistently into his dark ones.

He was silent a moment. Then he said, gently: "Hit's all right." Then, in a still lower, deeper voice: "If there was anybody I could talk to about hit, hit would be you."

The color sprang into Isabel's face as she replied: "Oh, I'm only a stranger; I could n't expect you to."

Ten minutes later, he said: "All the land this side of Troublesome, for a mile or more, was my paw's, and my part, four or five hundred acres, lays along here, from the creek to the top of the ridge. My house, hit's just out of sight up yander. Me and Charlie and t' other boys stays down here a lot in crap time, and this summer they aim to help me get out a lot of timber—yellow poplar. See them tall trees that lifts their heads so high above t' others, along the ridge and all down the sides? There's a sight of 'em. And them hills are full of coal, too, five or six veins of hit."

When they arrived at Aunt Ailsie's, Isabel was much taken with the ancient log house—the great fireplace, with its pots, spiders, and kettles; the loom, the reel, and the spinning-wheels and "kivers." But Aunt Ailsie would not let her spend much time looking. She set them down to a half-past-ten o'clock dinner, in order, as she said, that they might have a "full evening" before them. By eleven-thirty the three were starting up the mountain in the rear of the house.

Cornfields extended halfway up, and were so steep and crumbly that Isabel had to be pulled up much of the way by Fult. He and Aunt Ailsie took the ascent like goats, but had to stop frequently for Isabel to recover her breath.

Up in the timber, it was equally steep, but there were bushes and limbs to hang on to, and also the ground was solid beneath their feet. At last, after many rests, they reached the high rocks, a hard formation giving a castellated appearance to this ridge and others that billowed away in the distance. Through a cleft in the rocks, Fult led the way, and, emerging on the far side, they found themselves under an overhanging shelf,—a "rock-house," Aunt Ailsie called it,—which was dry and comfortable, with some flat stones to sit on, and from which there was a glorious view.

Aunt Ailsie was pretty nervous. "Get out on top and take a far look around afore I begin," she said to Fult.

When he returned, she removed her black sun-bonnet, laid it on her lap, and inquired: "What'll I start with?"

"I already sung 'Turkish Lady' and 'Barbary Allen' and one or two more for her," he said. "The older they are, the better she likes them—them old way-back ones that come over from old England and Scotland long time ago."

"Yes," said Isabel, with enthusiasm; "think of finding one eight hundred years old, like 'Turkish Lady'!"

"Well, I'll sing you them my old granny teached me," said Aunt Ailsie. "I ricollect one has your name in hit; 'Lady Isabel and the Elf Knight' is hits name."

She began in a high-pitched voice, to a weird minor tune:—

"Lady Isabel sets in her bower a-sewing,
   All as the gowans grow gay,
Then she hears an Elf Knight his horn a-blowing,
   The first morning in May."

Enchanted by the magic strains, Lady Isabel makes a wish that she might possess both the horn and its blower. Whereupon the Elf Knight leaps into her window, seizes her, and takes her on his horse far away into the deep greenwood, only to inform her on arriving there that he has already slain seven king's daughters on that spot, and that she shall be the eighth.

She pleads for a moment of happiness first, begging him to sit down and rest his head on her knee for a little while before she dies. He does so; she strokes his head, weaves a spell over him, and lulls him to sleep; then binds him with his sword-belt and plunges a "dag-dirk" into his heart, bidding him lie there and be a husband to the seven slain women.

The next ballad was a many-stanzaed one, "Lord Thomas and Fair Ellender":—

"'O mother, O mother, come riddle my sport,
Come riddle it all as one,
Must I go marry Fair Ellender,
Or bring the Brown Girl home?'

"'The Brown Girl she has houses and lands,
Fair Ellender she has none;
I charge you on my blessing, Lord Thomas,
Go bring the Brown Girl home.'

"'Go saddle up my milk-white steed,
Go saddle him up for me;
I'll go and invite Fair Ellender
My wedding for to see.'

"He rode, he rode, till he came to the Hall;
He tingled all on the ring;
Nobody so ready as Fair Ellender herself
To rise and bid him come in.

"'What news, what news?' Fair Ellender cried;
'What news have you fetched to me?'
'I've come to invite thee to my wedding;
Is that good news for thee?'

"'Bad news, bad news,' Fair Ellender cried,
'Bad news have you fetched to me;
I once did think I would be your bride,
And you my bridegroom would be.'

"'O mother, O mother, come riddle my sport,
Come riddle it all as one;
Must I go to Lord Thomas's wedding,
Or tarry with thee at home?'

"'Oh, enemies, enemies, you have there;
The Brown Girl she has none;
I charge you on my blessing, fair daughter,
To tarry this day at home.'

"'There may be few of my friends, mother,
And many more of my foes;
But if I never return again,
To Lord Thomas's wedding I'll go.'

"She dressed herself in scarlet-red,
Her maidens she dressed in green,
And every town that she rode through
They took her to be some queen.

"She rode, she rode, till she came to the Hall;
She tingled all on the ring;
Nobody so ready as Lord Thomas himself
To rise and bid her come in.

"He took her by the lily-white hand,
He led her through the hall,
And set her down in a golden chair,
Among the ladies all.

"'Is this your bride,' Fair Ellender cried,
'That looks so wonderful brown?
You once could have married as fair a ladie
As ever the sun shone on!'

"'Despise her not, Fair Ellen,' he cried,
'Despise her not to me;
I'd rather have your little finger
Than her whole bodye.'

"The Brown Girl had a little pen-knife,

> It was both keen and sharp;
> Between the long ribs and the short,
> She pierced Fair Ellender's heart.
>
> "'Oh, what is the matter?' Lord Thomas, he cried.
> 'Oh, are you blind?' said she,
> 'And don't you see my own heart's blood
> Come trinkling down my knee?'
>
> "He seized the Brown Girl by the hand,
> And dragged her across the hall;
> He took a bright sword and cut off her head
> And flung it again' the wall.
>
> "'O mother, O mother, go dig my grave,
> Go dig hit both wide and deep,
> And lay Fair Ellender in my arms,
> And the Brown Girl at my feet.'
>
> "He placed the butt again' the wall,
> The p'int again' his heart.
> Did you ever see three true-lovers meet
> That had so soon to part?"

Then followed many another ancient ballad, passed down through the centuries by word of mouth in England and Scotland; brought across the seas, to be cherished in the rough pioneer days as reminders of the old home; and, later, forgotten in the stress of American life by the more fortunately placed, to become to the mountaineer, in his isolation, the sole outlet for imagination and fancy, the chief source of inspiration and ideals.

The tunes themselves were invariably minor, and weird beyond credence, harking back, most of them, to a time before the development of the present musical scale, when the primitive one then in use possessed only five notes.

All afternoon Isabel sat spellbound, listening to one long-buried tragedy after another, living back into the lives of her remote ancestors, when feeling was less restrained, love more ardent, hate and vengeance more swift and sure; when, also, the world was inhabited by more picturesque beings—lords, ladies, kings and queens.

Often Isabel had sighed for the days of romance and chivalry; believed she had been born out of time into a world prosaic, spiritless, commercial-minded; felt an impatience with the men she knew—Thomas Vance, for instance, who could be content to spend nine or ten hours of every day in his cashier's cage at the bank. She knew now that the old world of the ballads was the one to which she truly belonged.

Many times during the afternoon she glanced at Fult's face, impassive always, save for the smouldering eyes. Only once, when news of the cruel killing of a Douglas is brought to his castle, and his "baby son, on the nourice's knee," miraculously speaks up: "Gin I live to be a man, revenged I'll be," did she see a spasm of feeling pass over it.

Frequently, between ballads, Aunt Ailsie opened her closed eyes and sent Fult to the top of the rocks. During one of his absences on sentinel duty in the late afternoon, she surprised Isabel by saying: "But there's jest as good song-ballats made nowadays as there was in them old ancient times."

"What do you mean?"

"Why, there's men that follers making song-ballats about things that happens now, and does naught but set in chimley-corners and sing 'em, and nobody is welcomer wherever they go. There's two blind Beverly boys—but they hain't boys now no longer—that never did nothing else. They are kindly kin to the Fallons. I'll sing you some of theirn some day, about the wars in this country. After Fulty kilt Rafe Kent and was sont down to Frankfort, they made up one about the Fallon-Kent war and him."

Isabel was thrilled. "I must hear it," she said.

"I'd never dairst to sing hit in his hearing," replied Aunt Ailsie; "the onliest chanct would be to get him away a while."

"Oh, please do!" entreated Isabel, as Fult stepped back into the rock-house.

After another old ballad, Aunt Ailsie said:—

"Fulty, your grandpaw's been ailing a right smart with the rheumatiz in his j'ints, like you know, and I been a-wishing for some yaller-root to bile down for him. In the days when we follered digging sang through these hills, there was a sight of hit growed on this here mountain—beyand that next spur was a good place. There's time a-plenty yet,—Lot he won't never get back afore dark,—and if you feel to, you might go down and dig a few roots."

Fult rose with alacrity. "I will," he said, "if Miss Isabel will go with me."

He turned his handsome eyes upon her.

"She hain't hardly equal to sech a ja'nt yet a while. You go down-along by yourself, and me 'n' her 'll set and wait for you."

"Oh, come," pleaded Fult, insistently, with both voice and eyes.

"I suppose your grandmother is right—I had better not attempt too much climbing the first day," smiled Isabel.

Very reluctantly, Fult departed; and when he was at a safe distance, Aunt Ailsie began, in a low voice, the "Ballad of the Fallon-Kent War":—

"Come all young men and maidens fair
And hear a tale of trouble.
Take warning, boys, shun packing guns,
And likewise liquor's bubble.

"Red Rafe and Fighting Fult, when young,
Both follered driving cattle
Down to the level land; a word
Did plunge them into battle.

"Both being drunk, a brindle steer
Hit sarved as cause for quarrel;
The lie was give, then weepons drawed,
Then two smoking gun-bar'ls.

"Both being wounded bad, hate kept
A-working like slow pizen:
Each vowed that t'other he would kill
The minute he laid eyes on.

"Fult's friends was quick to take his part,
The Kent clan strong did rally,
And War hit fell on Troublesome
Like a land-slip down a valley.

"O Lord, I hate to tell the tale
Of all the woes that followed.
Twenty-five year in troubles sore
The county hit was swallowed.

"For both was men of high degree,
With office in the county;
Fult to the Jail-house held the key,
Rafe drawed the Sheriff's bounty.

"And more and more, as years went by,
Outsiders in hit mingled;
And worse and worse, each day, the war
With politics got tangled.

"See at the Forks the two sides meet,
At Christmas or Election.
The nags they plunge, the bullets whiz,
The guns they bark destruction.

"Beneath the beds the women-folks
And babes they go a-diving,
And all the folks that follers peace
In corners dark are hiving.

"Oh, hear the wounded yell, and see
The nags in franzy tromping
All on the dying men beneath,
Their foamy bits a-chomping.

"And now the battle's over, see

The dead lay cold and torn there,
And hear the women's shrieks and prayers
Upon the breezes borne there.

"Again, Rafe's crew besiege the Jail,
With many a shot and shell, sir;
Fult and his fighting men within,
They shorely give 'em hell, sir.

"Or maybe in the courthouse, when
The proof one side again' goes,
The war busts forth, and jury, judge,
And lawyers seek the windows.

"The years pass on, but not the hate;
Death keeps his toll a-taking;
Rafe's brothers two, and brothers' sons
And many more in-raking.

"And Fult his kin and friends sees die
For him, but still he lingers,
A rifle ever on his arm,
Three pistols nigh his fingers.

"They cannot whip him in fair fray,
So strategy they hatch up.
Rafe feigns to go a journey far,
A bad man for to catch up.

"Him and his men ride off by day,
But back by night they crawl, oh,
And hide away by the main road,
All in a spruce-pine hollow.

"Fult, breathing free at last, rides out,
His thoughts removed from danger;

Both mind and body take the rest
To which they are a stranger.

"He listens at the little birds
That sing the fair day's dawning.
O Fult, you better look around—
The grave for you is yawning!

"Too late, too late; unseen they dash
Upon him from the hollow;
A flash, a cry, and Fighting Fult
All in his gores doth wallow.

"The jury never dairst to bring
Again' Red Rafe a sentence;
On 'self-defense' he triumphed through,
Nor felt the first repentance.

"But where's Young Fult? By day and night
He's practising on gun-play,
And on his eighteenth birth, he rides
To meet Rafe, on a Sunday.

"He takes his life all in his hand;
He cares not for the danger,
All set upon the holy task
To be his paw's revenger.

"There in the open road they met,
All honest, fair and just, oh;
But Heaven aimed the bullet swift
That laid Rafe in the dust low.

"O Fulty, you've revenged your paw,
You've done your utmost duty;
No man can curl the lip of scorn

At you, in your young beauty.

"I know hit's hard on you to lay
And pine in Frankfort prison;
I'd ruther be there, though, admired,
Than safe home, in derision.

"The hearts of all is turnt to you
In love and fond affection;
And here we sing this ballad true
To keep you in recollection."

When, a moment later, Fult, alert, graceful, perfect in physical beauty, came in sight, moving rapidly up through the thick timber below, Isabel felt as if, in his person, Romance itself, beloved of the ages, wept, honored, and sung, was advancing swiftly toward her from out the veils and shadows of bygone centuries.

VII

The Funeral Occasion

AFTER the first month of the women's stay on Troublesome, there was a change in their daily programme, on account of the beginning of the public-school term the fourth week in July.

The school at The Forks was taught by Giles Kent, Uncle Ephraim's grandson and Darcy's cousin—a quiet, studious young man, who had been all along the most voracious reader of the brought-on books. When his school opened, with nearly two hundred scholars of all ages, and grades from first to eighth, to instruct in the three *R's*, and only one pupil-assistant to help him, he was only too glad to have the women continue their singing, sewing, and cooking classes in connection with his work. Cynthia Fallon offered the use of two rooms in her hotel, opposite the schoolhouse; various citizens lent tables, chairs, a stove, and tinware; and the cooking teacher established herself in one hotel room, while in the other Amy, assisted by Isabel, taught sewing, Isabel also going over to the school-house every morning for an opening half-hour of singing. The kindergarten was still held on the hill all morning; and after school the young folks still gathered there for the play-hour, and often came up again after supper for a "sing."

This left the heads of the work—Amy and Virginia—with their afternoons free for their cherished plan of visiting every home in the county within a radius of ten or twelve miles. They intended, first, walking to all not farther than six miles; and, later, riding to more distant ones.

The only disadvantage about the new arrangement was that it provided no occupation for the young men, Fult and his crowd, and

Darcy and his, who had been so assiduous in their attendance upon cooking, sewing, and singing classes on the hill.

Uncle Ephraim was troubled. "Hit is bad," he said; "the onliest way to keep them boys civil is to keep 'em busy. They won't go to school, where they need to be, with their sorry store of larning; and soon as time gets to laying heavy on their hands, they'll likely go back to stilling and drinking and shooting. I hain't so afeared for Darcy—he's got his mind so sot on the cook, he's aiming to keep peace if he sees any chanct; but hit's ontelling what Fult's crowd may do."

Amy spoke to Fult on the subject the evening he brought Isabel back from hearing Aunt Ailsie sing the devil's ditties.

"It would distress us deeply," she said, "if you young men got into bad ways just because after to-day there's nothing more going on up here to keep you interested."

"Don't have no fears," he replied; "there'll be no drinking or shooting long as you women stay with us. As for me and Charlie and t' other boys, we have us a job of getting out timber down on my land; but we'll be in here reg'lar of an evening for the play-parties, and of a night for the sings, you can depend."

He was true to his word. In mid-afternoon he and his friends rode in from his farm a mile down Troublesome, and stayed on the hill until supper-time, coming up again an hour later for the singing; and when the rest of the crowd left at eight, Fult always made some excuse to remain for an additional half hour—usually it was to teach Isabel a new ballad. Darcy Kent often lingered a while, too, talking with the cooking teacher; but the two enemies apparently never saw each other at such times.

There was a period in mid-morning when Amy taught the old folks on the shady hotel-porch, and when Isabel had nothing to do. On Thursday of the first week, she was in the sewing-room, writing letters home. She was in the midst of one to Thomas Vance, giving a graphic account of the young feud leader and his dash and charm,—she always told Thomas everything,—when voices on the back porch penetrated to her consciousness. Cynthia Fallon was saying, in her sharp tones:—

"No, Lethie don't never go up the hill to the play-parties no more, and hit's no wonder!"

Aunt Ailsie, who had evidently finished her primer lesson and joined her daughter for a while, replied: "She allowed to me, that day I started on my A B C's, that hit was her clothes—she said they looked so quare atter the singing gal come in, she did n't aim to shame Fulty by playing pardners with him no more. She said she'd give nigh her life to have some clothes that sot as good on her as the singing gal's."

"Clothes!" jeered Cynthia; "The reason she hain't been on that hill for nigh two weeks is because Fulty hain't never seed her nor heared her nor thought of her sence that air singing gal come in. He's pure franzied about her—hain't got eyes nor years for nobody else, and done forgot Lethie time out of mind. Man-like," she added, bitterly; "hit's allus the newest face with them. Hit was with his paw. And, of course, there's allus females laying wait to take 'em from their rightful women."

"The singing gal hain't one of 'em," spoke up Aunt Ailsie, with warmth; "I'll be bound she hain't got no idee Fulty and Lethie been a-talking for nigh two year, and would have married afore now if Lethie'd a-been minded to leave her paw's young-uns. Or else she don't see Fulty's manœuvres. Not that he likely means anything by hit; and I don't know as a body can blame him for liking pretty people—I like 'em myself. And as for Fighting Fult, Cynthy, if you had a-just helt yourself in, and been kindly blind-like, and not give him a tongue-lash every time he cast a seeing eye on a fair-looker, hit's my opinion life would have run a sight smoother for both, and he would n't have done the wandering he done. Faulting a man kindly aggs him on, 'pears like."

"Yes, lay hit all on me!" exclaimed Cynthia, angrily.

Isabel, shocked at what she had heard,—for though she had seen Lethie on the hill the first day or two, noticed her devotion to her baby brother, and been struck by her beauty, she had not known that Lethie and Fult were sweethearts, or been aware of her later absence,—rose at once, and went straight across the street to Madison Lee's store, and up the stairway on the outside.

A startled, but smiling Lethie, with little Madison in her arms, answered her knock and invited her in.

"I can't stay just now," said Isabel; "I ran over just between classes, to ask why you don't come over to our sewing lessons? The older girls are learning to make simple dresses now, and I believe you would like that, would n't you? And I would so gladly help you, not only in class but at other times; for I know how busy you must be kept with your father's house and all the children on your hands. Suppose we run down right now to your father's store and pick out a dress, and maybe I'll have time to cut it out before I leave."

"Oh, yes!" exclaimed Lethie, her large gray eyes starry; "oh, nobody knows how I have pined for pretty frocks; but I never knowed how to make 'em."

She looked down apologetically at her faded blue cotton dress.

"And another thing," smiled Isabel: "you must have not only sewing lessons, but singing lessons—special ones, all by yourself. For since you and Fult are sweethearts, and to be married some day, and he is so very fond of music,—of course that is why he has been on the hill so much,—it is your duty to learn the things that will give him happiness. And now let's go down and find the dress."

From a miscellaneous stock of saddles, bridles, ploughshares, hardware, salt, coffee, sugar, crackers, and stick candy in glass jars, they finally extracted several bolts of gingham and calico, and selected the prettiest. Going up again, Isabel quickly cut out the dress, and pinned it on Lethie.

"I'll run up again and finish this after dinner," she said, "and to-morrow you can begin another in class. I wonder, Lethie, if you know how pretty you are? You ought to be dressed in silks and gossamers all the time, like a fairy princess."

A rosy flush dyed Lethie's milk-white skin. "I never had no looks," she said. "You are the one that's pretty—the prettiest ever I seed!"

"In a beauty-show I'd never for an instant hold a candle to you," said Isabel. "Do you mind taking your hair down and letting me see it before I go?"

Lethie unfastened the large knot tightly drawn to the back of her head, and her beautiful pale gold hair fell in a thick shower, almost to her knees.

"Truly a fairy princess!" said Isabel. "Now do you mind if I put it up for you as a fairy princess ought to wear hers?"

She plaited the shining tresses in two large braids, and, leaving the hair loose and waving about Lethie's face, wound the braids about her head coronet-fashion, then held the child off, and gazed at her.

"Lethie," she said, "when I go home, I'm going to take you with me and astonish the Blue Grass with your beauty. I mean it!" as Lethie looked at her breathless. "From this day I'm going to adopt you for a younger sister, and see that your looks are properly set off."

As soon as dinner was over, Isabel returned to work on the dress, and by four it was finished and on Lethie, as were also a pair of Isabel's white canvas shoes and white stockings. Before the two started up the hill together, Lethie gazed at her reflection in the little looking-glass on the porch, with a loudly beating heart.

Isabel managed to see Fult before the playing began.

"Lethie is here to-day," she said; "and must be your partner the first time, and at least half the others."

So Lethie was made happy again by seeing Fult come to claim her. And she was no longer afraid of shaming him. Joy flushed her cheeks. She hoped he would say something about her changed appearance; but when he seemed abstracted and failed to, she was not deeply disappointed. Her unselfish heart demanded very little. To be near him, and to catch Isabel's reassuring smile across the circle, filled her cup.

That evening after the "sing," when the others, Charlie and Charlotta, Thad and Ruby and Lethie were starting down, and Fult, banjo in hand, prepared to linger, Isabel told him that she would be too busy about other things to learn ballads that night, and he must hurry down with the others. He went, with a darkened brow.

The following days brought to him always the same bafflement. Isabel was as friendly and smiling as ever, but never by any chance or effort could he see her alone; Lethie was always on hand, and Isabel was especially solicitous, even affectionate, toward her.

He waited, however, in expectation of the ride they were to have together on Sunday, to a funeral occasion over on Clinch. Several of the women, and some of the young folks from the village, were going in a party, for the first time deserting the Sunday School, which was to be conducted that day by just the kindergartner and the nurse, with Giles Kent's assistance.

The pleasure of the women in the trip was marred, however, by some shooting in the village the night before—the first since they had been settled on the hill. The nurse, coming up early in the morning, after sitting up with Polly Ainslee, who had typhoid, reported that it was not done by Fult and his crowd, as the women had at first feared, but by some of the very young boys, who had in some way gotten whiskey.

"Bob Ainslee came in the room where his mother was half dead with fever, and shot several times into the ceiling and then fell over on the other bed, too drunk to sit up," she said. "I wonder who is giving those boys liquor?"

When they went down to the hotel to mount their nags, Virginia spoke of the disturbance to Fult.

"I was so afraid at first it was your crowd," she said, "and so very thankful to hear it was n't."

Fult flushed. "Had you forgot what I done to Charlie the Fourth of July?" he asked.

"I did n't really think you'd fail us," she said. "I wonder where those poor boys, Bob and the others, are getting whiskey?"

"I reckon they could find hit up most any hollow, now the corn is laid by," he said. "They ought to have sense enough not to take too much."

He had already noticed, and felt some surprise over the fact, that Lethie was in the crowd, saying her farewells to little Madison, who was to be kept by Cynthia Fallon. He knew that he had not asked her, or provided the nag. Silently he helped her, and the others, into their side-saddles; and, as soon as they had started, began to manœuvre so that he and Isabel should fall behind. But in vain. Nothing could detach her from Lethie's side.

After following Left Fork of Troublesome for a few miles, they went up a smaller branch, and then crossed a mountain. As they reached the "gap" in the ridge and looked down on the far side, a faint thread of song came up to them from the valley, increasing in volume as they descended; until, as they reached the burying-ground, on a little rise beside the creek, it became a rich, minor, hauntingly beautiful chorus of men's voices.

Hundreds of people were already gathered, some seated on rows of planks laid across logs in the shade, others wandering about on the outskirts. There were a number of small, latticed grave-houses; and with their backs to these, and facing the crowd, sat five preachers, on a special plank under a spreading beech.

When the party from The Forks took seats on a rear plank, Fult achieved a seat beside Isabel, only to have her, at the last moment, change, leaving Lethie between them. She did not see the angry glance he turned upon her.

As they were seated, the singing ceased, and one of the preachers, an old man with a kind face, arose and announced that this crowd was "mustered" and this meeting held for the purpose of "doing up" the funerals of four deceased persons—Elhannon Bowles, who had passed away the previous summer with the fever; his month-old child, who had died the year before; his old father, dead five years; and his mother, dead eight years.

Short biographies were then given of the four, beginning with the infant child, who had "gone home to glory with the choking-disease afore sin had ever smirched the whiteness of hits soul"; of the old father, who had "drapped dead all unthoughted" one day in the cornfield, ill-prepared, it was to be feared, for what awaited him; of the old mother, who had "allus fit the good fight, and passed on a-shouting"; and, finally, of Elhannon, whose future status would have been shrouded in some doubt had it not been for a vision of a "shining nag," which brightened his last moments and left hope in the bosoms of his bereaved widow and seven orphant offsprings.

"Yes, Ardely," he said, addressing the widow, who, in black sunbonnet and dress, occupied the front plank with her seven small children and a disconsolate-looking man, "you have a right hope of j'ining Elhannon again in the land where there hain't no widows or orphants, no sorrow or no parting or no tears, no fever or no choking-disease. Yes, I know all about hit, Ardely—twicet have I been along the lonesome road you now tread; twicet was I called upon to part with a fond companion, and to be paw and maw to my younguns; two good women have I got in glory, and one in this mortal spere. I know how to sympathize with all widows, having been twicet a lonelie widow myself, and a fair prospect, my present companion being puny-turned, of walking yet again in that vale of tears. Yes, Ardely, nobody knows better than me what hit is to have the heartstrings tore and frazzled, and the light of day everly put out, by affliction."

The widow bowed her head and wept loudly beneath the black sunbonnet, and the seven off-springs laid their heads on her lap or on one another's shoulders and joined in the lament, as did also a number of black-bonneted women on the front seats.

With the words, "I feel to take the hand of every widow here, man or woman, that has ever lost a dear companion," the preacher, stepping forward, offered a consoling hand, first to Ardelia, and then to all the other bereaved ones who pressed forward, the women weeping, the men silent, but with working faces, to clasp the understanding hands of one who could enter into the fellowship of their sufferings. The spectacle of human loss and sorrow, always a poignant one, was relieved and softened by the outpouring of this old man's sympathy and love.

With tears trickling down his own cheeks, the preacher then returned to his place, to begin, in a breathless singsong, a minute history of the death-bed scenes of his two companions. During these recitations, the weeping on all sides increased, to such an extent that he was again impelled to come forward and shake hands all around to assuage the storm of feeling he had raised.

After returning to his place this time, it was with a different voice and manner that he spoke—sternly, and to the point.

"Hiram," he said, addressing the dejected-looking young man who sat with the widow and children, "hit now remains my duty to speak a few words of counsel and admonishment to you. Ardely here, not being able, as no lone woman is, to keep food in the mouths of seven young-uns and several head of property, tuck and married you at corn-planting time in Aprile, so's to have a man to make the crap for her. Hit is a mighty solemn thing for a man to take upon hisself sech a yoke as you have, and it behooves you often to examinate yourself and study on whether you are doing right by Elhannon's widow and orphants. Keep Elhannon's memory green, ricollect that, as him and you is now husbands-in-law, you must one day give account, not only to God Almighty, but to Elhannon hisself, for how you done his woman and young-uns. Elhannon allus had what might be called a fiery natur,' and onless he's changed a sight, I'd hate to be in your shoes and face him, Hiram, on the Day of Judgment, if I did n't have a clear bill of quittance writ in the Book of Life. You allus was, as far as I knowed, a well-intended boy, and never done much meanness, and I hope you never will do no more.

"And now, people, I will give way, and take my seat, as there's four more preachers sp'iling for a chanct to talk. Will one of the brethering line out the old hime-tune, 'My head and stay is called away.'"

Again the volume of song, rich, minor, beautiful, rolled forth, and this time the "lined out" words were plainly audible:—

"My head and stay is called away
And I am left alone.
My husband dear, who was so near,
Is fled away and gone.

"Hit breaks my heart, 't is hard to part
With one who was so kind.
Where shall I go to ease my smart,
Or heal my troubled mind?

"Naught can I find to ease my mind
In things which are below,
For earthly toys but vex my joys
And aggravate my woe."

Nothing could have been better than the new husband's solemn, self-effacing manner during the singing. Not only did he appear entirely reconciled to being a "mere earthly toy," and playing second fiddle to Elhannon in both time and eternity, but also he seemed solicitous not to "aggravate" Ardelia's woe in any possible way.

The next preacher then flung off his coat and launched into a vigorous exposition of the controversy between predestination and free will, which lasted for two hours. Many of the younger folks, and older ones, too, would quietly rise and take a rest-cure by promenading around through the trees for a while; but the real Old Primitives up in front, among them Uncle Lot, sat rapt and immovable throughout, strong doctrine being very meat and drink to their souls.

A third preacher discoursed for an hour upon the four beasts of Daniel's vision; a fourth for another hour upon nothing in particular;

a fifth in his talk took a fling at "this here new-fangled, fotched-on notion of Sunday Schools, which fine-haired furriners has brung amongst us, and which I defy 'em to find mentioned from one eend of the Bible to t'other." In the discourses of the last four preachers, there were two things in common—each took a special singsong and preached to it, and not one of the four referred in the slightest way to the occasion for the meeting, or to any of the deceased persons.

Before the meeting broke, at three o'clock, the invitation was extended to all and singular to come to dinner with Ardelia, who had "cooked up" for a week, and was ready for all comers.

Much as the party from The Forks wanted to go to the dinner, they felt that it was too late. They mingled with the crowd for a short while, talking and handshaking, and hearing from various persons that it had been a "pretty meeting." Then, half-famished, they fell upon the lunch they had brought with them, and, as soon as possible afterward, started homeward.

Fult helped Isabel on her nag last of all, and in a low voice, with handsome, imploring eyes, begged her to let the others ride on and wait a minute for him.

She said, "All right," and called out: "Lethie, come back—Mr. Fallon wants us to wait a minute for him."

Fult, flinging himself on his nag, darted a furious glance at her. A dark flush mounted to his very forehead. He rode beside the two girls in silence a few minutes, then quickened the pace until the three had caught up with the others. Just before the ascent of the mountain began, he jumped down, saying something about Isabel's saddle-girth, and did something to it, she could not see what.

He remounted, and they rode on as before, along the road as it wound around the lower part of the mountain. Then suddenly, at the first steep ascent, Isabel felt her girth give, her saddle slip from under her, and clutched wildly at her horse's mane.

Fult was at hand, and caught her before she could fall to the ground.

"Girt's broke," he said, "I allowed hit was n't very safe. Anybody got a stout string, or a piece of ground-hog hide?"

Nobody had. "I'll have to ride back to that house nigh the burying-ground and get some," he said. "The rest of you go right on;

you too, Lethie,—hit's getting late,—and me and Miss Isabel will catch up with you in just a little grain."

The others, including Lethie, rode on; and Isabel sat on a small bank alongside the road and waited for Fult, who was delayed somewhat longer than she had expected. At last he rode up, waving a string of ground-hog hide in his hand.

"Had to wait to cut the string off the hide," he explained.

He drew the saddle up on the bank beside her, and began to work at the girth. She watched him idly for a while, then suddenly leaned forward and took the girth from his hands.

"This girth was cut, not worn," she said, in an astonished voice.

Fult laughed, "Are you just finding hit out?" he said.

"What do you mean?" she demanded.

"You seed me get off and fix hit back there?"

"Yes," said Isabel, puzzled.

"Well, I cut hit then," he said, "nigh in two, not quite."

"You cut it—why?"

With anger gathering in his eyes, he dropped knife and string and slowly faced her. "Because," he said, "I've stood being treated this way as long as I aim to. For four days you hain't hardly looked at me or spoke to me; and when I try to talk to you, or sing to you, you all the time drag somebody else in,—Lethie or somebody,—so I don't never get a chance to be with you like I want to. And I'm tired of hit. I aim to talk to you, whether or no." His eyes blazed, his chest heaved.

"I don't think I just understand you," Isabel replied.

"Yes, you do," he exclaimed, angrily. "You seed, from the minute I laid eyes on you in that wagon down Troublesome, how things was with me—how I was plumb crazy about you, could n't stay away from you a minute hardly, or get you off my mind day or night. You knowed hit as well as I did."

"I did not," replied Isabel, slowly. "I knew, or hoped, that you liked me, because I liked you immensely; but I did n't imagine that it was—the other thing."

"You was bound to," cried Fult. "Hit was there plain in my heart and my eyes for you to see. Hit would n't be possible for me to feel so much and you not know hit."

"I was n't thinking of such matters. I came up here to work, not to have love-affairs. And, another thing, I did n't know anything about you and Lethie being sweethearts, or maybe I would have been more careful not to let you be with me so much."

"I thought that was hit," exulted Fult; "I allowed somebody had been telling you tales."

"No," said Isabel; "I simply overheard someone say how you had changed to Lethie; and then, of course, I was distressed to death over being a possible cause of suffering to her. It is really best, perhaps, that you and I should have this talk, and understand each other plainly. I want you to know that I won't permit this feeling you say you have for me to go on, or be spoken about, or even thought of. You must put it instantly out of your mind, unless you want me to leave for home tomorrow; for I'll never stay here and be the cause of suffering to that beautiful child, who already carries so many burdens. Of course she is the one you truly love, deep down in your heart; you have loved her truly, have n't you?"

"I loved her all right, or thought I did, till you come in; then she seemed to me just like you said,—a child,—and I knowed you was the woman for me, the one I had allus heared tell of in song-ballats, and had drempt about all my life. I knowed hit the minute I seed you setting there in the wagon in the middle of Troublesome, with the sunlight sifting down on your hair."

"It was because I was something new and strange," said Isabel. "People have these infatuations, but they don't amount to anything, they don't last. You'll get over it and wonder how you ever could have looked at me. I'm a most ordinary everyday person, but Lethie is beautiful, body and soul."

"Your looks suit me all right," said Fult, shortly. "You said a minute back you liked me immensely. Did you mean hit?"

"I meant just what I said, and no more: *like,* not love," said Isabel, firmly.

"Well," demanded Fult, tensely, "is there anybody else you *do* love?"

An unexpected thought of Thomas Vance crossed

Isabel's mind, only to be carelessly dismissed. "I can answer you truly, I am not in love with any man; I don't think I am the falling-in-love kind."

Fult veiled a triumphant gleam in his eyes. "Hit's all I want to know," he said. "If you don't already love nobody else, you can learn to love me."

Isabel answered sharply: "Of one thing you may be sure—I'd never let myself love a man who changes so easily as you do, and can be willing to treat a girl as you would treat Lethie."

Fult laughed, as if highly amused. "I'd never change to *you*," he said, with conviction; "I'd never treat *you* no way but right." Then, leaning toward her with pleading eyes, he said: "I hain't so hard to love, am I?"

Isabel rose. "I have told you what I shall do if you persist in this," she said.

Fult smiled. "I'd foller you down to the level land if you went," he declared. "Hit would n't make any difference to me where you was. I don't know but what I'd like hit better down there, without so many people around all the time."

"There would be my father and mother," said Isabel; "and I can tell you they would be very far from approving of you."

"Why?" demanded Fult, in a tone of surprise.

"Because of the wild and reckless things you have done."

Fult threw back his head and laughed aloud.

"Do you allow that would make any difference to me?" he asked. "I would n't ax nobody for my wife—if she liked me, I'd take her in the teeth of all the devils of hell! You mind how Earl Brand, and the Elf Knight, and all them other old-time fellows in the ballats done? Well, that's my way. I don't know but what I'd enjoy hit better if I did have to steal you!"

"Mr. Fallon," said Isabel, with dignity, "I see it is useless for us to talk further. Finish the girth and put the saddle on for me, please, and I'll ride on, and get my things together to start home to-morrow."

Fult reached up and gripped her wrist till it hurt.

"Do you think you can get away from me that way?" he said fiercely. "Don't you know I allus have what I want before I finish? That nothing can't stop me?"

The next instant, however, he was another man, calm, gentle, smiling. He released her hand, with the words: "I don't want to bother you none, though, or make you go home. Stay another week, and try me. I'll do like you say—be just friends. I got a lot to do this week, getting out timber, and maybe I can kindly work you off my mind."

"I don't doubt you can if you try," said Isabel; "I'll give you the chance, anyhow. You see, I know I am very much needed in the work here, and really don't want to leave."

He helped her into the saddle, and they rode on as rapidly as possible, in the effort to catch up with the crowd.

VIII

Moonshine

THE night of the women's return from the funeral occasion, there was again some shooting down in the village, as there had been the night previous; and the women feared that Billy Lee was one of the culprits, as Lethie came up in his place to milk their cow next morning.

They were much troubled; and as Uncle Ephraim Kent, on account of rheumatism, was unable to come to his reading lesson Monday morning, Amy and Virginia, accompanied by Isabel, went across Troublesome after dinner, to consult with him on the subject. The Kent lands extended for a mile or two along the far side of the creek, and Uncle Ephraim's home was in a hollow opposite the village. They crossed on a long footlog, which was chained to a great water-elm on Uncle Ephraim's bank, so that it should not be entirely carried away by "tides."

The old man was sitting just inside the doorway of his ancient log house, trousers rolled up, and his legs, from the knee down, bound in red flannel. His wife placed chairs. It was Isabel's first visit to his home, and her eyes flew at once to the long old muzzle-loading rifle and the strange musical instrument that hung over his "fireboard." and as soon as possible she asked him about them.

The rifle, it appeared, had been the one used by his "grandsir," the old Cap'n, when he "fit under Washington"; the dulcimer he himself had made when a young man courting his first wife (the present one was his second).

"Dulcimores," he said, "used to be the onliest music in this country; the knowledge how to make 'em and pick on 'em was fotched in by our forebears. But banjos and fiddles has nigh run 'em out now."

At Isabel's urging, he picked a tune on the old dulcimer, laying it across his knees and using two quills, one to "note" with, and one to pick with. The music was like the droning of a million mosquitoes.

He said that the old musket was still in use in his young days—that he had killed many a deer with it. "Allus in them days I follered wearing red, because hit makes the deer stand at gaze. And"—pointing to the crimson linsey hunting-jacket that hung on a peg by the door—"I'm still a-wearing hit, though there hain't been a deer seed in these parts for allus. In them early days I never bothered with no shoes, or even moccasins—the soles of my feet was so thick I could easy crush chestnut-burrs with 'em. And many's the time I have laid out all night in the pouring rain and never kotched ary cold. Present-day young folks hain't no account—they have tendered their-selves too much."

He also had his wife get out from a chest his greatest treasure—his grandsir's old yellow, crumbling Bible, "fotched out in his saddle-bags when he come acrost from Old Virginny. And which now," he said triumphantly, "I can read myself, nigh as good as him."

So saying, he opened the faded pages at the Twenty-third Psalm, and, with some prompting from Amy at the hard words, read it through proudly.

The women then broached the subject of their visit—the shooting in the village the past two nights.

"I heared hit all," said the old man. "Hit hain't Fult and his crowd, or Darcy and his'n, thank God! but just some of the sprouting-age boys that has got hold of liquor some way, and tuck too much."

"But where do they get the liquor?"

Uncle Ephraim shook his head. "No deeficulty about that," he said. "Stilling most gen'ally starts up pretty prompt atter the crap is laid by. You see, the folks in this country mostly feels they have got a fair right to do what pleases 'em with their corn they have raised, law or no law, and that the Gover'ment hain't got no business meddling. And I don't know but what they got right and jestice on their side, so fur as right and jestice goes. But what I look at is, the devilish harm the liquor does. Casting an eye back over a long lifetime, and the awful wickedness of men, and the general meanness of their manœuvres, I can't hardly ricollect a wrong that did n't have whiskey behind hit or mixed up in hit. The infamious stuff!" he cried, leaning forward in his chair with clenched hands, "hit ought to be buried face downward, unfathomed deep, and writ over the grave, 'No reesurrection'!"

Settling back in his chair after a moment, he continued, in a different voice: "Folks is allus a-counseling me, 'Take a leetle corn-liquor for your rheumatiz'; hit's the holpingest medicine ever was made.' And so hit may be. But I'd sooner stand the pain as to pour that devil's potion down my neck. Now don't you get tore up in your minds over them boys, women. I'll ax around and try to get on the track of where they're getting that liquor."

In the evening, just before the "sing," the women spoke to Fult about the trouble.

"Them boys need to have their necks broke for drinking too much and disturbing your peace that way," he said; "they ought to know when to stop. If I'd a-been in town, I'd a learnt 'em. Hit won't happen no more; I'll put fear in 'em before I leave."

Sure enough, it did not happen again that week, and the women's fears were laid to rest.

So, also, were Isabel's. Fult's behavior toward her during the week was perfect. When he and his crowd rode in from the farm for the late afternoon play-parties, he was friendly and pleasant, chose Lethie and herself impartially for his partners, made no effort whatever to see her alone, either then or after the evening "sings," and did not permit himself so much as a glance that would trouble her. Occasionally he and his friends would be absent at one or the other time; but usually they were on hand, as were also Darcy and his crowd; and the women congratulated themselves that the young men, the dangerous element, were keeping entirely out of trouble.

Every afternoon the heads of the work, Virginia and Amy, continued their walks, visiting the homes up all the creeks and branches within a radius of five or six miles, often not returning until nearly dark. On account of helping with the play-parties in the afternoon and conducting the sings in the evening, Isabel could not join these expeditions, much as she longed to. But when she learned that they proposed going up Noah's Run Saturday afternoon, she declared she would for once desert duty and go along. The previous Saturday a woman from the head of that branch had visited the hill, with a tiny, withered baby in a black calico dress with white polka dots, and the appearance of the poor little creature had so wrought upon Isabel that she determined to follow it up.

Saturday morning she hastily made a little dress and cap from one of her own pretty petticoats, bought the remainder of a very primitive baby outfit down in the village, and was ready to start with the other two women after dinner.

They followed Troublesome for a couple of miles, then turned up the winding branch that bore the name, Noah's Run. Less than a mile from its mouth was a small store, with nags tied to limbs outside, and men sitting on the puncheon benches in front. The storekeeper's home, a neat, weatherboarded house, was the first visited. The wife welcomed the women as old friends, having visited them on the hill, and her nine children also having attended the classes pretty regularly. They asked her, among other things, if typhoid had as yet appeared up her branch; there were already two or three cases of it in the village, where it seemed to be expected as confidently as the coming of summer. She said it had not yet begun on Noah's Run, though everybody was looking for it any day.

"Everybody on the branch is a-trying to stave hit off by dosting up on corn-liquor. A dram all around is what me and my man and all our young-uns takes of a morning and of a night."

To their suggestions that drinking-water be boiled and flies be kept away from food, she was impervious. "Corn-liquor's the shorest way," she said.

Hers was the only house on the branch which had a window, the others being all windowless log cabins.

At the first of these, the mother, fat, flabby, and dirty, claimed to have been unable to visit the hill because of poor health. "I got the breast complaint—some calls hit the galloping consumpt," she informed them, proudly.

She sat complacently on the small, rotting porch, fanning herself with a turkey-wing, while a dozen tow-headed children (boys wearing a single garment,—a cotton shirt,—girls in ragged cotton dresses) gathered around to stare with steady, unblinking eyes at the strangers; and numerous chickens and ducks, and a large litter of young pigs wandered at will through porch and house.

"I have heared a sight about you quare women, and have longed to lay eyes on you," the invalid said. "The quarest thing I heared was that not nary one of you had a man."

They admitted the truth of this rumor, and she gave them another searching inspection, remarking afterward: "Don't none of you appear to be pining, though—I allow you have got past hit. I've heared old maids has a mighty happy time when they git through strugglin.'"

What did she do for her "breast complaint"? Well, a nip of corn-liquor was the "clearingest" thing known for breast and neck. Was it hard to get? Oh, not now, since the crap was laid by.

Were her children in school? No, indeed, there was n't any school to go to on Noah's Run—never had been. She would like to see her boys get larning—hit holped a man along; but as for gals, she herself had got on without any, and she allowed women were in general better off without it. "Not meaning no disrespect to you that have got hit," she hastened to add. "But you see yourself how hit is—a woman that sets out to ketch larning is mighty apt not to ketch her a man."

On the porch of the next cabin stood a great loom and two spinning wheels. The woman of the house was out in the middle of the branch, washing wool by treading it in a loose basket. She let down her skirts, dried her hands on her apron, and hurried toward the guests, taking them through a clean-swept yard into a clean-swept cabin. Everything was clean—the floor, the chairs, the three fat beds in the room, the broad hearth, her own gnarled hands and striped homespun dress and apron, the shirts of her boys, the faded dresses of her girls. She said she had only seven children at home now, her "main oldest" boy having died a few years back, and her three oldest girls having married. She said this oldest boy had been a "pure scholar"; that although he had never "sot in a schoolhouse" a day in his life, he had in some way got hold of a speller, and taught himself his letters, and before he was through, could spell every word in the book, backwards or forwards, and knew all the reading the same way. If he had lived, it was "ontelling" what heights he would have climbed to.

"Davy there, my thirteen-year-old, he has the like ambition," she said, pointing to a boy whose fine, intelligent face flushed under their gaze. "He'll larn, someway or 'nother, though I don't know how; for, though there's a big mess of young-uns on this branch, there hain't a sign of a school, nor likely to be, 'pears like."

One of the younger boys lay across the foot of one of the beds, with his throat tied up. "He follers having the quinzy," said his mother.

To the question, "What do you do for him?" she replied: "We make him set and rest frequent at corn-hoeing time, and I give him a little corn-liquor to kindly help him up when hit's handy. He's a smart-turned child, too—all my young-uns is, if they could jest get a chanst."

The next cabin was that of a young pair only three years married, but in this time they had done their utmost in the way of replenishing the earth, as three "least ones" attested. The home following was that of a pair of grandparents, who, having raised one large family, had now started again with eight orphan grandchildren. They and the mother of thirteen in the next cabin expressed fervent wishes that their young should have a chance at learning; and in reply to the question as to what they were doing to prevent typhoid, responded, as others had done, that a little grain of corn-liquor was the best preventive known.

So far, the women had counted fifty-two children on the branch. In the next house there were eleven; and the home of the black calico baby, at the head of the branch, four miles from its mouth, remained to be visited.

Arriving there, they saw the mother beside the branch, "battling" the clothes she had just washed and boiled in a big iron kettle. She would lift them out of the kettle, lay them on a smooth stump, and then beat, or "battle," them with a flat stick. Evidently washboards were an unknown luxury up Noah's Run.

She came forward with joy when she saw the visitors. The wizened baby, still in the black calico dress and a very dirty cap, lay on a pallet beneath a big apple tree, with a swarm of flies hovering over it, which an old, old woman who sat by, smoking a pipe, dispersed every now and then with a leafy switch. She took the pipe from her mouth to gaze at the strangers with all her might.

"Is them the quare women, Phronie?" she asked.

"Hit is," replied Phronie.

"That hain't got ary man amongst 'em?"

"The same," replied Phronie; then, to the visitors, "This here is my maw's old granny that lives with me; she's terrible old—I allow nigh a hunderd. She don't like to live with none of her grands but me."

"Stop talking and set cheers for 'em, Phronie," commanded the old lady, sharply.

Whereupon Phronie went into the house and fetched out two chairs, which, with the one the grandmother sat upon, appeared to be the entire stock. When the other two visitors were seated, Isabel, picking up the poor little baby, from whose eyes the experience and suffering of ages looked out, took her seat on a convenient tree-root, whither the other children, who had scattered like rabbits on the appearance of the women, slowly gathered—nine besides the baby.

Here the old lady, with the remark, "I was about to forgit my manners," made a sudden dive into her pocket and brought forth a cob pipe similar to the one she was smoking, and a twist of tobacco, handing them to Virginia, with the invitation, "Take a smoke."

"Thank you," said Virginia, "but I don't smoke."

"Don't you now? Well, that's quare—I'd larn hit if I was you. My ole granny used to look so pretty a-smoking, I kotched hit from her, same as I kotched my trade."

"She follers doctoring women when their time comes," explained Phronie.

"Me and my ole granny together has brung very nigh all the babes that come to this country for a hunderd year," boasted the old woman. "But, women, if you don't smoke, take a chaw."

"No, thanks, I believe not."

The old soul looked crestfallen. "I allow you foller chawing manufact,' and this here hain't nothing but home-made," she apologized.

"No, I should prefer this to manufactured if I took it at all," Virginia assured her; and to Phronie she said: "Tell us more about your baby. How old is it?"

"Well, women," said Phronie, in a surprised tone, "I don't rightly know. Hit were borned quite a spell before corn-crapping time—about three or four week, were n't hit, granny?"

"Nigher five," granny replied. "I ricollect hit by the dark of the moon."

"Then it's around four months old?"

"I reckon. But hit hain't growed none sence the day hit come."

"Has it been sick?"

"No, hit don't appear to be—never hollers or cries none; I never seed a civiler baby. Hit jest lays and pines and pindles."

"Do you nurse it yourself?"

"Give hit suck, you mean? Yes, I allus have a plenty for two young-uns. And hit'll mostly take the teat all right, but will jest kindly mouth hit, and not suck hearty like t' other young-uns."

"What do you do for it?"

"Nary thing on earth but give hit good corn-liquor reg'lar. I seed from the start hit was puny-like, and commenced right off dosting hit generous, four or five times a day, to help up its stren'th and wake up hit's appetite."

"To help up hit's stren'th and wake up hit's appetite," echoed the old granny, in her high, cracked voice; "hain't nothing like good corn-liquor, for young or old."

"And hit was hard to get, too, at corn-crapping time," complained Phronie; "but," virtuously, "I allus managed to get some."

"If I were you, I would not give it any more," said Amy. "Doctors nowadays say it is very bad for babies, and stunts their growth and poisons them badly. Suppose you try for a couple of weeks not giving it any."

Phronie and granny looked at her in open-mouthed amazement.

"Phronie," said the old lady at last, "these here quare women has got a sight of book-larning, and if they was to spend their opinions on books, I'd listen at 'em. But what does a passel of old maids, that hain't got a baby to their names, know about babies?"

Phronie's objection was on a different ground. "Hit would look too mean," she said, "for me to drink hit myself and not give none to my child."

"Try leaving it off yourself, and see if your milk won't agree better with the baby," suggested Virginia.

But the old lady spoke authoritatively: "Hain't nothing like liquor for nursing mothers."

The women were silenced. But Isabel opened her bundle and exhibited the things she had brought for the baby, and asked if she might give it a warm bath and dress it up.

Phronie immediately set things going. Two of the boys were ordered to chop wood and make up again the fire under the big kettle, another to draw water from the well; one of the little girls ran for the family towel, another for the soft soap, another for the dishpan. And there, under the apple tree, in the dishpan, Isabel gave the poor little skeleton baby the first comfortable bath it had ever had in its life, drying it afterward, not with the soiled, stiff family towel, but with one of the soft rags she had brought. She bathed it, all but its head—for on this point granny and Phronie were adamant. To wash a babe's head, or leave off its cap, under a year, was certain death. "And I love my child too good to run ary risk," said Phronie. The best Isabel could do was to put the clean cap on the dirty little head.

The small creature looked up at her gratefully out of its age-old eyes, and rewarded her by going to sleep in her arms.

Phronie insisted that the women should stay to supper, the afternoon being about gone. They had brought sandwiches with them in case of a late return, but accepted her invitation.

Four or five of the children then ran down a chicken, which Phronie killed and fried. She also warmed up a pot of string beans, and made biscuits and coffee, and the visitors sat down to a plentiful supper, occupying the three chairs, while Ben, Phronie's husband, sat on the churn, and the nine children, not greedy and grabbing as most would have been, but always quiet and "civil," stood and ate. The women felt it to be a shame that such well-behaved and apparently bright children should be six miles away from a schoolhouse, and entirely cut off from opportunity.

When the guests were ready to start home, Phronie said there was a "nigher" way for them to return by than the one they had taken coming—that the walk might be shortened two miles by going along the ridge-tops. This idea appealed—they knew it could not get very dark, because the full moon would be rising too soon. So Ben took them up the mountain in the rear, and a short way along the ridge, leaving them with the directions: "All you got to do is to keep to the main ridge, whichever way hit winds, and not turn off on no spur; and hit'll fetch you right out over them cloth houses of yourn. And there hain't no varmints to bother you, less'n hit is a few rattle-snakes, which, if you don't step on 'em, won't do you no harm."

The sun had long since set, but they went along in the clear evening light, with an exhilarating view of other ridges stretching off on every side. Along the ridge-top was a narrow, hard-rock formation, which had resisted the wear and tear of ages, and which made a good, clear path, and lifted them pretty well above the timber, save where a great yellow poplar thrust its giant head up, here and there. In the narrow valleys below, mist was already gathering. Pale stars came out, and steadily brightened; but the women walked on in the dusk, unafraid.

At last, after they had gone on for an hour, Virginia exclaimed: "I think I know where we are now. To the right is the valley of Troublesome, and the land below us must be Fallon's, where Fult and his friends are getting out timber. And oh, there's the flush in the east where the moon is rising!"

An instant later, Isabel exclaimed, "Is n't that a light down in the timber just ahead of us?"

"Yes, it certainly is; probably Fult and the boys are having a 'possum hunt."

"It seems to be a steady glow, not a moving lantern."

"Well, a 'possum supper, then."

They went on in silence, keeping an eye on the light, which was now just below them, apparently at the base of the rock, or cliff, they were on. Then they heard the murmur of voices. A thick curtain of grapevine here hung in and between the trees, so that in the daytime vision could never have penetrated to what was beneath. But now, through the interstices, they could plainly see, about thirty feet below them, the steady glow of a large fire, which appeared to be under a sort of furnace of rock; a number of planks and barrels; several rifles leaning against a tree; and some of Fult's crowd of young men. Four were engaged in a game of cards, by the light of the furnace; another was watching the game and feeding the furnace with an occasional chunk of wood; still another was working at the barrels; while the last—Charlie Lee—was sampling the tiny stream that trickled from a pipe in the barrel nearest the furnace and fell into a bucket. Fult himself was nowhere to be seen.

"These boys are not having any 'possum supper," said Virginia, in a shocked voice; "they are running a still."

"Oh, they could n't," exclaimed Amy, "after all Fult's promises to us."

"I've been wild to see a still all my life," said Isabel.

The three stood rooted, gazing with all their eyes. As they looked, Fult himself, rifle on arm (evidently he had been on guard below), stepped into the circle of light.

"Mend up the fire, boys," he ordered, "we want to finish this last run-off. Hit ought to be nigh done now. Charlie, quit tasting them strong shots—you hain't able to stand hit."

Stooping over, he tasted a "shot" himself, to tell about the stage of the liquor. At the same moment, Isabel, in her consuming desire to see the fuller workings of the still, stepped nearer to the cliff-edge, and with her foot struck a small rock, scarcely more than a pebble, which bounded off the cliff. It could not have made much noise in falling; but instantly the furnace light was completely muffled, every voice was stilled. Then, before any of the women could stir, a bullet whizzed just over Isabel's head, and a sharp command of "Halt!" rang out. There was the sound of someone scrambling up through trees and vines, and in another instant Fult, rifle in hand, stepped out on the cliff before them, into the moonlight.

He looked, and stood as if turned to stone.

For a long moment nobody spoke. Then Amy found her voice.

"We were spending the afternoon on Noah's Run," she said, "and the people kept us to supper and sent us back the near way, over the ridges. We saw the light, and wondered what it could be, and stopped to see."

"I allow you found out," laughed Fult, unpleasantly.

"We did; but with no intention of spying. We did not dream you would do such a thing as run a still."

"I never drempt either hit could be you women, or I would n't have shot when I heared the rock fall, and seed a head again' the sky-line."

"I suppose you have forgotten all your promises to us," said Virginia sadly.

"I hain't broke a single promise to you," replied Fult, indignantly. "I don't break my word. Nary one of my crowd hain't done a bit of drinking or shooting yet, or broke the peace in any way."

"But the liquor you are making?"

"Hit ain't for this country. I aim to take hit to the Virginny line and sell hit there at the mines, where I can get a good price."

"But you did let some of the younger boys get hold of some, did n't you?"

"I give a jug unthoughted to Bob Ainslee for going an arrand, never thinking of him and t' other young boys getting drunk on hit."

"Oh, why do you do these things which distress us so, and which are directly against the law?" implored Amy.

"Laws hain't nothing to me if they're onjust," he declared, defiantly. "I don't think hit's wrong to use the corn I have raised in stilling liquor, or I would n't do hit. But," in a changed and troubled voice, "I would n't have had you women see this still for a thousand dollars."

"Why?"

"Oh, because you look at things different from me. You have got strange notions. You don't understand our ways up here."

He cast a desperate, searching glance into Isabel's face, as if in the wild hope of finding some understanding and sympathy there. But her eyes were dropped; her body was drooping somewhat wearily.

There seemed nothing more to be said on either side. The women turned slowly away and began their homeward walk.

"Won't—won't you let me—or Charlie—see you safe home?" Fult asked, in a choked voice.

"No, we feel safer alone, thank you," replied Virginia.

And they walked on, leaving Fult standing like a statue in the moonlight.

Three hours later, the six women on the hill were awakened from slumber by the most frightful sounds—rapid shooting, hard galloping, blood-curdling whoops and yells—down in the village street; and knew only too well that Fult and his crowd had drunk deeply and ridden in to "shoot up" the town. Compared with this, the scattering shots of the previous Saturday and Sunday nights had been but feeble child's-play. For an hour, death and destruction seemed to be let loose. The women lay trembling in their tents, hoping against hope that no one would be killed, feeling that their summer's work had been utterly in vain; while down in the village mothers crawled under beds with their children, and lay flattened against the floor, to dodge the flying bullets.

Every person in the village sought safety but one. That one was Lethie. Directly over the street where the frenzied boys dashed back and forth, she knelt by her window, following Fult's figure in wild apprehension and terror, and sending up incoherent prayers for his safety. It was nights such as this which had saddened and aged the child beyond her years.

IX

The Danger Line

THE morning after the shooting-up of the village by Fult and his friends, Billy Lee, when he came up to milk the pieded heifer, brought the welcome news to the women that nobody had been killed, or even hurt, but Polly Ainslee's old sow. "The boys allus shoots mostly in the air, and if folks lays on the floor there hain't no danger," he said. "I hain't never afeared myself; but Lethie—hit's a sight how hit skeers her."

The children who came up later to Sunday School corroborated his statements. "Gee-oh! hit was like old times," they said.

Darcy Kent also spoke of it. "Of course I knowed just what hit was," he said to them, "and if it had been anybody else, I'd have come down the creek and settled 'em; but having give my word to you about the truce, I could n't, for hit would have brought on the war again at hits worst."

"Yes, you did the only wise thing," they agreed.

He gazed frowningly down the valley. "Fallons is outlaws," he said, "and allus was, and allus will be, long as one of 'em lives. The only way is to hunt 'em down like dogs; which my family, being sheriffs for many a year, and defenders and upholders of the law, has tried hard to do."

He turned away with Annette, the cooking teacher, his tawny hair and handsome yellow eyes making an attractive contrast to her silky black hair and blue eyes.

"Oh, don't ever try to do anything to them again," she said with a shudder, as they went down the spur; "whatever Fult does, let him alone. I could n't have stood it last night if I had thought you were there."

He flushed. "If I ever did give up the war entirely," he said in a low voice, "hit would be for your sake—because you wanted me to live."

"I do, I do," she replied. "You *must* live—for me!"

"You are sure of yourself now?"

"Yes, I found out last night, when I was so frightened for fear you might be down there. Remember, you have me to think of now," she said.

All that day the women, with the exception of Annette, were profoundly depressed. Though it was only the first week in August, and they had planned to stay until September, they felt that it would be just as well to pack up and leave at once. They almost wished they had not come; for their affections were now entwined and rooted in a community for which they could do nothing.

A larger crowd than usual climbed the hill to the vesper service that evening, many of the older people, as well as the young. Uncle Ephraim was one.

"I allowed you would be out of heart, atter last night," he said, "and limped up along to holp up your sperrits. Hit hain't right ever to expect too much of human natur,' which is a pore, puny, failable contraption at best. Them boys has sp'ilt the summer for us; but I allow by now they feel as bad as anybody about hit. And ricollect, the worst hain't happened—the war hain't started again. I was afeared you might take a notion to leave; but I feel to counsel you to have patience, and stay on with us, and trust in the Lord."

The vesper service was a sad affair—nobody could put much spirit into the singing, or reading, or prayers. Then, suddenly, Uncle Ephraim, in his quavering old voice, raised the words of the ancient hymn, "How firm a foundation," to the quaint but impressive mountain tune; and then depression seemed to flee away, courage and faith to return; real fervor was poured into the song.

As the words of the last verse rolled out over the hills, all unseen to the worshipers a small group of men came down the spur from the ridge top, and stood in the thick shade until the people had all started down the slope. The women, gathered at Pulpit Rock, were about to follow, when the group advanced in a body and stood before them, and they saw with amazement Fult and his friends.

"Women," he said, and in the dusk his eyes looked very large and dark against the pallor of his face, "I allow the sight of us won't be a welcome one to you no more; but anyhow we come, soon as we was fully at ourselves, and knowed what had happened, to tell you how we feel over last night.

"When you found us working at the still, we was doing just like I told you, getting out timber of a day, but also, of a night, stilling us some liquor to take to Virginny and sell there; not one of us had n't broke our word to you about drinking and disturbing the peace, nor never aimed to. But though you had no cause, women, you said a hard word to me as you was leaving, when, not liking to see lone women wander by theirselves of a night, I axed if one of us could n't see you home. You said no, you felt safer alone.

"Women, that word pierced my heart like a pizened arrow, and rankled till hit put me plumb beyond myself, and in a pure franzy. Long as you trusted me, I could n't disapp'int you; but when you did n't, nothing never mattered—I never cared no more what I done. When I got down off the rock, I drank me a pint of strong liquor; and t' other boys, seeing me, and hearing what you had said, done the same. Before long, we was crazy as lunatics, and I don't ricollect nothing more; but I heared from Billy Lee, when he brung our dinner down to us, that we had rid in and shot up the town again.

"I was mighty sorry to hear hit, women,—all of us was,—and mighty glad to hear nobody was n't killed but Polly Ainslee's old sow.

"So we come in to-night to tell you how we feel about hit, and to ax you not to let hit put you in the notion to leave. If you allow you'd ruther not stay here with us boys around,—which I would n't blame you much atter what we done last night,—I come to tell you we'll all light out immediate for Virginny, with our liquor, and not come back till you've gone. Or, if you feel to put your trust in us one more time, and give us a chance to right ourselves, we'll pour out every bit and grain of that whiskey, and not make nor drink nary 'nother drap long as you stay here.

"And to show you we mean what we say, women, I have brung along with me, and, if you say so, am now aiming to turn over to you to keep while you stay, something we can't make no liquor without, something we set a sight of store by; for"—lifting from the ground at his feet a shining coil of copper pipe, and passing caressing hands over it—"hit's the finest worm in Knott County, and the onliest one I got."

There was not the slightest hesitation on the part of the women. Amy put out her arms for the worm. Virginia spoke eagerly: "Certainly we'll trust you again; and for my part I deeply regret the words I spoke to you last night, and apologize for them. Forgive me, and I'll never fail to trust your word again. And we'll take the best care of the worm, and I'll tell the people how things are, and everything will be all right."

So things began to flow peacefully again on Troublesome, and the women entered upon the last three weeks of their stay. Every day Amy and Virginia walked or rode up different creeks or branches, visiting the homes, visiting also the district schools, few and far between, within which, too often, teacher and boys spat tobacco juice over the filthy floors, and the pupils, with their only textbook—a blue-back speller—in hand, wandered from one rude bench to another, talking or studying aloud, or even fighting, at will.

Every day, too, the nurse brought hope and healing to the sick, especially to the typhoid cases that had recently started in the village. And every day Isabel, Annette, and the kindergartner, after their regular duties were over, worked busily upon plans for the closing entertainment on the hill, to which the county should be invited. Besides songs, Isabel had in mind various tableaux from old ballads and folk-tales, which should fill hungry eyes with pretty colors and sights, and bring before the actual vision scenes long familiar to the imagination. She had already written home for pieces of velvet and silk and cheesecloth of many colors, and also for a very beautiful dress she had recently worn as bridesmaid, and which was now designed for special use in connection with Lethie.

After his reinstatement in the good graces of the women, Fult seemed somewhat chastened, walked softly, obeyed their slightest wish, and made himself unobtrusively useful. To Lethie, when she was on the hill, he was kind, though abstracted; to Isabel his conduct was in every way so perfect that she almost forgot the day of the funeral occasion. But for the fact that a slight veil of melancholy appeared always to envelop him, he would have seemed the same as before.

So laid at rest were her fears, so full of other things the busy days, that when, one afternoon, not ten days before they were leaving, he came up the hill soon after dinner, banjo in hand, saying he had a new ballad to teach her if she wished to learn it, she went unhesitatingly to the spur-top with him, and sat on a bench beneath a spreading beech. He took his seat on the ground before her, and began the plaintive ballad. It was a long-drawn-out, doleful, but beautiful one about misplaced love, with the oft-recurring refrain:—

If I had known, before I courted,
That love was such a sorrowful thing,
I'd have locked my heart in a box of golden,
And pinned it down with a silver pin.

As he sang, he lifted dark, mournful eyes to hers; and toward the end, she was amazed to see them brimmed with tears. Tears in Fult's eyes seemed to her the strangest sight she had ever looked upon.

"You see hit hain't no use," he said, very gently, dashing away the tears before they could overflow. "To pleasure you, I try not to show what I feel; but hit hurts, hurts me, all the time."

Isabel said, as lightly as she could, "You just imagine it hurts; you'll forget before I'm out of sight."

"I'll never forget," declared Fult, in a low voice; "hit would n't be possible. Allus I'll keep you in my mind, and carry your picture in my heart; long as I live hit'll be the same, even though I don't never see you or hear of you ever again. You are going far away from me, where I won't never hear your sweet voice no more, or look upon your face with delight. But even if the old salt sea was to roll forever between us, my feelings for you would still be the same; I could n't never change."

This new mood of his, sad, earnest, gentle, undemanding, worked upon Isabel's sympathies; the thought of being hopelessly loved by such a beautiful being smote her romantic soul.

"I wish I had never come," she said, "if my coming meant even a little suffering for you."

"Oh, no," he replied, with a martyr's look, "I'd rather suffer torments as not to have loved you; the pain of hit is better than any other pleasure. And as long as you stay where I can get a look at you now and then, I can stand hit all right; but now you are fixing to go away where I won't never, never see you no more, hit appears to be more than I can face."

Then, suddenly, as a distressed child might have done, he bowed his head on his hands, and his body shook with sobs.

It was a beautiful head, of noble shape, with glossy, blue-black hair. Isabel's heart was torn as she gazed upon his grief. For an instant she forgot everything but his suffering.

"Don't take it this way," she begged, and there were tears now in her own eyes. "I never dreamed you cared really, and it distresses me to death."

Fult made no reply save to give her a long look; then he sat, head bowed in hands, body shaken with slow sobs, for some minutes. At last, lifting mournful eyes to hers, he asked, gently, hopelessly:—

"If you and me had met away off somewheres in some far and distant land, where there was n't no Lethie or nothing to come between us, do you allow then you could maybe have loved me the same as I love you?"

Isabel replied, in a voice she tried to make calm: "Almost any girl would find it an easy thing to fall in love with you."

"Not 'almost any girl,' but you," he persisted, gently.

"I—I don't know about it," answered Isabel; "I never thought that far along. You see, there *were* things between us,—Lethie and other things besides,—and that was enough for me, as I told you the day of the funeral meeting. And it's not any use to discuss the matter now. We must be going back down the hill."

"Must be going back down the hill," Fult repeated, sadly. He rose to his feet.

"Good-bye," he said in a low voice, still gazing with deep sadness into her eyes.

"Good-bye," she said, with a catch in her voice, putting forth her hand; "I hope we shall always be friends."

Taking her hand, he raised it to his lips and kissed it, slowly, reverently, as one might kiss the hands of the beloved dead. No knight of old—not Sir Philip Sidney himself—could have done the thing more perfectly. Isabel was much moved. Two large tears rolled down from her eyes and splashed on his wrist.

Then, as she turned away, he suddenly seized her hand again with both of his own, and covered it with kisses, but this time they were wild, hungry, passionate.

Isabel broke from him and ran down the hill; but in the instant of her flight he saw in her face the things he had hoped and planned to see—not only pity and pain, but also very real fear of herself.

After this the days flew; with rehearsals for the entertainment, work on costumes and the like, every waking moment of Isabel's time was occupied; and, though Fult was on hand most of the time, helping in every possible way, he did not again make the least effort to see her alone, or refer in any way to their conversation on the hill.

It was the custom of Isabel, Annette, and the kindergarten teacher, every night after the rehearsals, to go down to the kitchen tent and get something to eat before retiring. Thursday night of the last week Isabel, coming out of the door as the three were about to leave after eating, had an impression of a head vanishing round the tent corner. The shadows of the trees were too dark, however, for her to be at all certain, and, putting it down to weariness and nerves, she dismissed the matter from her mind.

Then came the last busy Saturday; the entertainment was to be on the following Monday, and the women were to start out of the mountains on Tuesday. Amy and Virginia had ridden nearly thirty miles that day, visiting homes on a distant creek, and, coming in about dark, had gone immediately to their tent and to bed. Isabel shared this tent with them, but it was much later before she could get to bed: rehearsals, all sorts of last things, were to be attended to. At last it was over, and she, Annette, and the kindergartner, as was their custom, went down after the departing guests to the kitchen tent. They set the lantern on the kitchen table, and ate by its light. Then Isabel, being unusually tired, dropped down on the bench just outside the door to rest, while the other two put away the food and dishes.

She had hardly sat down when she felt something thrown and tightened over her mouth, and, attempting to cry out, realized that she was gagged and unable to utter a sound. The next instant she was lifted by a pair of strong arms and borne swiftly away. The next, Fult's voice spoke low in her ear: "Hit is me—don't take no fear." Then, as she fought and struggled desperately: "I would n't fight if I was you; hit will only mean I'll have to tie your hands and feet." When she struggled and fought all the more violently, he set her down, swiftly knotted a leather strap about her wrists, and, as she made a wild pass to run, stooped and fastened another around her ankles. "Hit's too bad," he said, calmly, "to have to tie you up this way; I hate to do it, but hit's the only way. I allowed you'd fight, and was ready for hit. Soon as them women go up the hill, we'll mount the nag and start for Hazard."

The whole thing had happened with great swiftness and in complete silence. The two other women were now going up the hill with the lantern; not thirty feet from them, Isabel heard Annette say, "She was so tired, she has gone on up ahead of us to bed," and was unable to move or make a sound.

Fult waited until they were safely inside their tent. Then he said, exultantly, to Isabel: "Did you actually think for one minute I'd ever let you go away and not marry me? That I was n't no more of a man than to fold my hands and give you up? You never knowed me, if you did—I don't allow nothing to stand between me and my desire. All the time I aimed to have you; all the time, knowing you'd never go of your free will, on account of Lethie, I planned to take you same as the Elf Knight took Lady Isabel, or Earl Brand, or them other men of old, took their true loves; and ever sence that day on the hill, when I made you show you liked me a little, I've been just watching my chance. Three nights I've laid wait here by the kitchen tent. And now I've got you, we'll ride to Hazard and get our license, and be married by sun-up."

Again Isabel struggled and fought with desperation, bound as she was. Fult held her in a grip of iron. "Fight on till you tire," he laughed. "I'm able to stand hit. Hit may scare you and hurt your feelings a little grain to be took off like this, but hit's the onliest way for your happiness and mine, and some day you'll thank me."

When she was exhausted, he picked her up again, saying, "I've got to carry you down now a piece to where the nag is," and strode swiftly down to where, by the light of a moon almost hidden by clouds, they could see his mare tied to a bush.

Leaping into the saddle, and sitting far back himself, he pulled Isabel up, gagged and bound, placing her before him as one would hold a child. "I hain't taking no chances on letting you set behind," he said; "you might throw yourself off and get bad hurt."

The mare picked her way slowly at first down the steep hollow, till they came out behind the courthouse. Then Fult put spur to her, and she sprang ahead like a flash, past the courthouse, across the street, down the dark lane between Madison Lee's store and the schoolhouse, and into the creek. The only light they saw in the village was a dim one in Lethie's window.

Along the creek they went plunging, past the back yards of the village on one side, and Uncle Ephraim's steep slopes on the other. When they came to the end of the town, Fult turned the mare into the road again alongside the creek, and slowed the pace. "We got the night before us to make the twenty mile," he said; "we'll get there long before the county clerk is up, anyhow; no use to kill the mare."

And Isabel? First there had been in her mind fear—hideous, panic, choking fear; and when that was somewhat abated, she was held for a long time as in a nightmare, every faculty paralyzed by the shock of the situation in which she found herself. The thing that was being done was unthinkable, impossible; yet it was happening, and she was powerless as a baby to prevent it.

Then she began making desperate efforts to gather her wits together, to grasp the situation and in some way deal with it.

She saw that Fult must have taken her emotion that day on the hill for a sign she loved him; and indeed, for a moment, sympathy and pity had led her pretty near the danger-line. Always her romantic temperament had drawn her into difficulties; but none that could be compared with this. Never before had she come across a man who dared to deal with matters in Fult's masterful and high-handed fashion. And she could not blame him—what he was doing he believed to be for her happiness quite as much as his own, and he was merely carrying it out in the simple and time-honored fashion of the old ballads he was always singing. Had the consequences not been so dreadful all round, his daring might have appealed to her.

But with Lethie broken in heart and life by the treachery of the two she loved and trusted; with her parents stricken and horrified when this bolt from out the blue should fall upon them; with the community hating her forever as the destroyer of Lethie's happiness; with the reproach that would be brought upon the whole summer's work of the women through this mad act—for of course no one would ever believe that she had been taken against her will; with the misery that was sure to result for Fult as well as for herself, since she did not love him and was not at all fitted for the life he could give her; the whole affair was fraught with terrible danger and calamity, and something must be done at once,—before it was forever too late,—to prevent its further carrying out.

But what to do? How, bound mouth, hands and feet as she was, to make her feeling known to Fult, to turn him from his wild purpose, and persuade him to take her back before the night was yet over, and the news of their going had become known? He would never give over his purpose if she was unable to speak until they reached the next county-seat and the clerk's office in the morning, and the escapade had become public property. His pride would not permit that. Whatever was to be done must be done at once, for they were traveling at a swift pace, and the time must be past midnight.

Desperately she cast about in her mind for a plan; still more desperately she realized that she had none—was all at sea. She was not used to getting herself out of her difficulties—it was Thomas Vance who always did that. She had always, since babyhood, taken her troubles to him; and always he knew a way out for her. She felt confident that, if he were only at hand, he could help her out of this. She even had a feeling that, if she could call to him, he would hear her, two hundred miles away, and save her.

Suddenly she had a perfectly overwhelming longing for Thomas, he was such an old stand-by—the one thing she knew she could always count upon, though, of course, he laughed at her a good deal; ever since she grew up he had been content to play the part of elder brother, to hear all about her love-affairs and problems, and give her advice and counsel: pretty magnanimous of him if he really cared for her himself as he professed to do. Of course she had never thought of being in love with him; she had known him too long and well. Love, she had believed, would be something strange, unimagined, unknown, and its object some hero, all fire, romance, and beauty, who would one day drop from the skies and claim her. Well, here was the unimagined, the unknown, the romantic, with a vengeance,—a perfect cyclone of it,—and in the very midst of it, swept on by its relentless power, she was sighing, longing, desperately praying for just one moment of the accustomed, the ordinary, the known and tried—in short, for Thomas. She would have given her life for just one reassuring tone of his voice, one touch of his hand on her arm, one glance from his humorous, dependable brown eyes, even if they were laughing at her.

Suddenly the need of him became so poignant, so desperate, that she began to call upon him, to cry out for him, just as if her voice could really carry through those two hundred miles of space; the want became a delirium, a frenzy, the muffled cries more wild and sharp; violently, without restraint, she shook and sobbed in Fult's arms.

Her storm of distress finally brought Fult to a halt.

"I allow the straps are hurting you," he said; "or maybe you are cramped. I reckon there's time for us to walk a piece; I'll take the strap off your feet and we'll walk a while, if you say so."

She nodded vehement acquiescence.

He dropped her gently from the mare's back, got off himself, and unfastened the strap from her ankles. Together they walked along the road, he leading the mare with one hand and steadying Isabel with the other. The moon, though not bright, gave light enough for them to see by, except in some denser shadows of the trees.

The relief of having her feet free was immense. Struggling with a mighty effort for self-control, she ceased sobbing, and after a while motioned for him to take off the gag.

At first he seemed unwilling, then said: "Hit could n't hurt none, though; there hain't a human being in two or three mile to hear you if you was to holler. And I reckon I'm able to stand what you have to say to me about Lethie. Of course, I know you'll have a plenty."

With difficulty he untied the gag, and Isabel drew great, gasping breaths of air into her lungs.

"I allow your wrists had better stay tied," he said. "They don't hurt you much, do they?"

"No," replied Isabel.

She walked on beside him, submitting meekly to his guiding hand on her arm, and not uttering one word of reproach. Her silence continued—became so prolonged and unnatural that Fult began to be troubled. He would rather have heard upbraidings.

"Hain't you got a word to say to me?" he asked at last. "Not a word for the man that loves you better than life, and has broke through everything to get you?"

She did not answer at once. Then she said, faintly: "Yes, I have things to say, but my mind does n't seem to work very well; I seem to need time."

Fult laughed low. "Take all you want," he said. "I aim to give you everything you ever call for, and never to cross you noway."

For quite a distance they walked on, through dim patches of shadow and brighter spots of moon-light. Finally, as with a great effort, she spoke.

"You—you believed I was in love with you that day on the hill when we had our last talk, and I ran away from you?"

Fult laughed a low, joyous laugh. "Hit looked that way—like you were afeared you might be."

"I *was* afraid—for a moment," she said. "I was all wrought up and troubled about you, and not quite myself."

"I knowed you never meant to show hit, never would unless you was compelled to some way; that was why I laid my plans to *make* you show hit—I felt like I ought to, before I took you off."

"You laid your plans to make me show it? How so?" she asked, in astonishment. "I fear I don't understand."

He laughed easily. "Oh, nothing; just by working on your feelings a little grain."

"Working on my feelings? When?"

"That last day on the hill."

"When you sang to me, and showed such sorrow at giving me up?"

"Yes," he said.

"Do you mean to say you were not really sad or suffering that day—that you put it all on, just to see the effect on me?"

"How could I be sad and suffering," he asked, "when I never for one minute aimed to be parted from you, or to give you up? I had my plans fixed even then to take you." He laughed delightedly. "But I allowed I'd just see how things really was with you, before I finally did."

Isabel stopped where she stood, in blank amazement.

"Do you mean to tell me it was just play-acting—all that moving scene?"

"All's fair in love and war," laughed Fult; "hit was n't play-acting about the way I loved you; but the rest I reckon was."

Her voice took on a new and stern note as she continued: "In other words, you deliberately deceived me and worked on my sympathy and got my feelings wrought up? Those tears you shed were crocodile tears, those heart-broken words and looks were all just a piece of fine acting?"

"I allowed myself hit was pretty well done," replied Fult, in a self-congratulatory tone.

"And you were entirely satisfied with the result of it?" Her voice now took on an edge.

"I was, too." Again he laughed the low, triumphant laugh.

"You were quite satisfied I loved you? It did n't occur to you that a moment of excitement and distress was not a reliable time to judge a person by?"

"What I saw was enough for me," he said. "I knowed if you loved me even a little, I could learn you to love me better and better."

"But suppose," said Isabel,—and her voice was hard and cold,—"suppose that you should be mistaken. Suppose I could never learn to love a man who deliberately deceives me, and then gloats over it. Suppose I did not love you in the first place and, after that, never could?"

Anger mounted in Fult's voice as he replied: "But I done hit all for you!"

"No, you did n't, you did it for your own sake, to gratify your vanity, I suppose. The very fact you could do it shows you cared nothing for me. Real love does n't deceive and play-act. And I'm glad I found out what you had done, because I had believed that you really were suffering, and it is a great relief to me to know that you were not, and that in reality you care nothing more for me than I do for you."

"But I *do* love you," cried Fult, furiously; "and you love me, too; you *have* to, when you're going to be my wife by sun-up!"

"Maybe I'm going to be your wife by sun-up,—maybe I can't help myself,—but if I am, it will be with anything but love in my heart."

Fult stopped in his tracks. "I won't hear you say that!" he cried, threateningly.

"I not only do not love you, but I do love another man," continued Isabel, standing straight and unabashed before him. "I found it out tonight—it all came over me like a flood when I believed I had lost him forever."

"Hit's a lie!" he exclaimed, savagely.

"It's the truth," she said, tensely. "It's someone I have known always; he lived on the next place to ours, we grew up together, he is as much a part of my life as breathing; but because I knew him so well, and believed love to be something strange, unknown, romantic, I did n't realize it was love I felt for him. I found it out to-night on this ride, when I wanted him above all things in the universe. He's not so picturesque or handsome as you are; but he's good, he's unselfish, he's true—he'd die rather than deceive anybody, or treat a girl as you have been willing to treat Lethie. And he's *mine*. And it was the thought of him, even more than of her, that broke my heart to-night."

Seizing Isabel by the shoulders, Fult shook her with such violence that all her joints seemed loosened. "Hush!" he commanded. "Don't drive me too far; I don't want to kill you!"

"I'm not at all afraid that you will," she replied. "That would n't mend matters."

"No other man shall ever have you!" he said between his teeth. His hand moved toward his pistol pocket.

She stood before him, calm, unflinching. "You are too much of a man for such talk as that," she said. "Let's try to look at things sensibly and see what can be done. You deceived yourself, and me, into thinking you cared for me, when in reality you did n't—your play-acting proves that. And because you saw I admired the old ballad-heroes and their ways, you thought it would please me to have you copy after them. Well, it did n't—it shocked me almost to death instead, and made me feel how cruel you were willing to be toward Lethie, and how selfish to destroy all the influence of our summer's work in this way. The whole thing, you see, has been just a mistake. But it may not be too late to retrieve it. Nobody knows that I am not asleep in my tent to-night; nobody will know before morning. If it is possible for us to ride back there by daybreak, not a soul will ever know, and no real harm will be done. If, on the contrary, we do not get back by morning, there will be a great hue and cry, your absence as well as mine will be discovered, they will put two and two together, and as much harm will be done as if we had actually been married. If you can possibly get me there, don't you think you had better take me back to The Forks at once?"

Fult looked at her fiercely. "I never took a back-track in my life," he said, chokingly.

"Do you want to marry me, knowing I love another man?"

"No, I would n't have you as a precious gift! But I aim to ride on—I don't know nor care where, so I never see you again. You get back the best way you can."

In another instant he had flung himself on the mare, and spurred her forward in great leaps.

Isabel was left entirely alone in the night, ten or eleven miles from The Forks. But, at least, she was free. She knew there was no possible chance of her reaching there before day; still, she would do her best. She turned and began to run along the road, and, when her breath was exhausted by this, to walk on as swiftly as possible.

Probably it was twenty minutes before she heard the beat of hoofs behind her, and then Fult's voice, saying, coldly: "I can't leave you this way; hit would n't be right. No use to have the talk about you, though, for my part, I don't care. Get on behind, and I'll try to get you back in time, though hit'll be a hard ride."

Taking off his coat, he spread it behind him, and rode up alongside a bank.

"I believed you'd think better of it," said Isabel.

Thankfully she jumped on, and grasped the hantle of the saddle. Thus had she ridden behind him the day he brought her up Troublesome into the village. Now they were to ride up Troublesome again, but in how different a manner!

With only the words, "Hold on, for hit's aiming to be the hardest ride you ever had," he turned the mare around, dashed the spurs into her side, and they were off, over rocks, roots, bowlders, up hill and down hill, through water above their stir-rups—on, on, with never a pause or a break in the wild gallop.

But always Isabel managed to hang on, though sometimes by the skin of her teeth; and always in her heart hope was singing—they would get there in time after all: Lethie's happiness was not to be destroyed, the summer's work was not to be made a reproach instead of a benefit, she herself was free, free—for Thomas. Fervently she prayed; thankfully she heard Fult urge on the wearying mare.

Finally, as there was the first lightening of the sky in the east, they turned up Fult's hollow, past his house, which she had never seen before, and almost straight up the mountain in the rear, as far as the panting horse could take them. Then Fult spoke.

"You could n't never get in by way of The Forks without somebody seeing you. But by taking to the ridge here, you can go along it and down the spur to the tents, without no danger."

He helped her down, turned the mare loose, and in silence they climbed to the high rocks and walked swiftly along the ridge—the same ridge where she and Amy and Virginia had discovered the still.

Dawn was rosy in the sky when they came out over the spur where the women's tents were, and stopped in the shelter of the trees.

"Go on by yourself now," said Fult; "there hain't nothing to hurt you. And I've got you here in time; I don't see nobody stirring."

Isabel turned to him, and held out her hand.

"Don't think I don't appreciate what you have done for me," she said. "I can never, never tell how grateful I am for your generosity. And I want to beg a favor of you. There are only two more days of our stay: be just the same you have been to us; don't let anyone see there is any change. You are a very important part of the entertainment on Monday, and if you are not there, it cannot go on. For everybody's sake, will you come?"

"I'll be there," he said, shortly. He turned and strode rapidly back along the ridge; and Isabel, slipping silently down the spur, entered the tent where Amy and Virginia were still sleeping, and crept into her cot without a sound.

X

Farewell to Summer

THE last day of the women's stay on Troublesome dawned bright and fair. Early in the morning the work of packing began, the smaller things being put in boxes and carried down the hill by Fult and his friends to the hotel, ready to be placed in wagons the following morning. Later, the tents were taken down and packed—all but one, which was to be used as a dressing-room for the "show" in the afternoon.

Aunt Ailsie came in early to help, as did also Charlotta and Ruby Fallon, Lethie, and others of the girls.

Between nine and ten the county people began to ride in in numbers. The women and children came on up the hill, but the men tarried in the village. For, all unknown to the quare women, Uncle Ephraim had had boys stationed at the three roads, requesting all the men to come to the courthouse to a meeting.

About eleven-thirty the men ascended the hill in a body, and joined their families for dinner. Aunt Ailsie had invited Amy and Virginia and the others to eat with her, and her capacious baskets held enough for forty people.

Numerous gifts also were brought in to the women on this last day—handsome large gourds, yarn mitts, turkey-wings for fans, hand-woven linen towels, and, from Aunt Ailsie, fine striped linsey petticoats for each of the six.

Shortly after dinner, the "show" began. A platform built just in front of Pulpit Rock, and closely curtained on four sides, aroused much curiosity, nothing in the nature of a dramatic entertainment ever having been seen before.

There was first a short speech of welcome by Giles Kent, the school-teacher; then songs by the children of different grades; then a short talk by the nurse on ways of preventing typhoid, tuberculosis, and other diseases; then marching and songs by the little kindergartners.

Afterward came the great feature and surprise of the day: a number of tableaux—scenes from old ballads and folk-tales, long known to the imaginations of the people, but here enacted before their eyes by the young folks in beautiful costumes.

Fult sang the ballads and, at the proper time, the curtains were drawn back and the scenes revealed. There were two from "Barbara Allen," three from "Jackaro," and two from "Turkish Lady"; the latter being especially striking, with Darcy Kent as the noble English captive and Charlotta Fallon as the Turkish Lady who sets him free and afterward follows him to his castle in England, where all ends happily.

Last came two incidents from "Lord Lovel" (this ballad was sung by Charlie, not by Fult). The hero, bound "strange countries for to see," bids farewell to the lovely Lady Nancibelle, and rides away on his milk-white steed (only it had to be changed to "coal-black," being Fult's mare, with Fult as rider). He returns, after a year and a day of wandering, to find the people all gathered around the bier of Lady Nancibelle, who has pined away and died of longing for him; and thereupon he himself dies of a broken heart. Annette took the part of the "lovely Lady Nancibelle," and Fult was beautiful in the velvet clothes and plumed hat of Lord Lovel.

Then followed several folk-tales, done by the children: Red Riding-Hood, Cinderella, and Blue-beard, the tales being told by Amy as the scenes were given.

And now came the surprise of the occasion—no one had known of it but Isabel and the performers: two tableaux from "The Sleeping Beauty."

The curtain opened with the young princess, under the spell of the wicked fairy, lying asleep, surrounded by the court people, and the king and queen on their thrones, all likewise sleeping. Lethie, in a rich robe of pink satin, with her pale golden hair falling over the dark velvet couch, was very lovely. But it was in the second scene, where the rince (Ronald Kent, a younger brother of Giles, a beautiful dark-eyed stripling) enters the court, kisses the princess, raises her to her feet, and leads her forward, that Lethie's full loveliness broke upon the assembly.

Standing there, the golden veil of her hair streaming down from a coronet of pearls over the rich, flowing folds of satin, her bare neck and arms white as their strings of pearls, her pale cheeks for once pink with excitement, her large eyes starry, her lips gravely smiling, she was a vision of delight. Women, children, men gazed spellbound. Never had they seen, or imagined, anything to compare with this. Her beauty was of the kind that brings tears to the eyes, a pang to the heart, because of its very perfection. And a spiritual quality shone through the fleshly vessel as a clear light in a vase of alabaster. People asked themselves if it were possible this was their Lethie; or was it in truth a fairy princess, a creature not of this earth?

Hidden behind the curtain, Isabel watched their faces, and particularly one face, that of Fult. Still wearing his velvet clothes and plumed hat, he stood near one side of the platform, his gaze fixed upon Lethie, in utter surprise and bewilderment; it was as if for the first time he really saw her. Then he leaned forward, to see better. Then he turned and saw the whole assembly hanging rapt upon her beauty. Then he looked again, excitedly, delightedly, with a proud air of proprietorship. His face flushed when he saw that Ronald continued to hold her hand.

Isabel remembered Cynthia Fallon's words,—"Hit's allus the newest face with them,"—and realized that she herself had been but an episode in Fult's life; that this wonderful new Lethie, super-imposed upon the old, was the girl who, if any girl could, would hold Fult's wild heart.

When the curtain was at last drawn over Lethie's loveliness, and the stage cleared, Amy and Virginia rose from the bench where they sat with Aunt Ailsie, and mounted the platform to say a few words of farewell to the people.

But Uncle Ephraim was ahead of them. "Women," he said, stepping up beside them, "don't speak the word 'far'well' yet—not till you listen at what we got to say." He began:—

"Women, citizens and friends, this here summer has been the ridge-top of my life, to which all my hopes and prayers and ambitions has p'inted. Hit has likewise been a Mount Nebo, to which I was led up for to gaze out upon the Promised Land. Being, like Moses, allus a man of prayer, I had faith to believe that some day the Lord would stretch out his mighty hand for our deliverance.

"So, people under my voice, hit was n't no great of a surprise to me when these here women come in. I seed in their coming the dawning of our hope, the gorrontee of our betterment, the asshorance that the Lord had brung us to remembrance. And all along, friends, hit has been in my mind that this summer wasn't noways the eend, but just the beginning of the blessings the Lord aimed to pour out on us.

"I never spoke to the women or to nobody; I just laid hit on the Lord and waited for his guiding hand. And when I heared the county was all a-mustering for a last day here, hit appeared like a coal of fire from the altar was toched to my lips, and I was commanded to speak out the words that would be put into my mouth. And though I hain't no speaker, and never was, I did n't dairst to deny the call.

"So, gethering the citizens together in the court-house, I spoke my thoughts, which was that somehow, I could n't say exactly how, we must fix to keep these women with us, to link 'em everly down to us; that, like the apostuls in the Good Book, we ought to be minded to build tabernacles for 'em, so's they would allus abide with us.

"And about that time Giles, my grandson, riz and tuck the words out of my mouth, to say that what was needed was to make the women stay and start up a right school; that, good as his intentions was, he knowed well he was n't noways able to do for the young-uns what the women could; and anyhow he was minded to go down in the level land and get more larning soon as he could be spared. Which right there, friends, I rej'iced to feel that my mantle had fell on Giles.

"Then one atter another of the citizens spoke, and the gineral sense of the meeting appeared to be that we could n't noway part with these women; and that, if somehow or 'nother they could be brung round to stay and start up a school, hit would be the best day that ever riz on Knott County.

"Then we got down to rael business and talked about hows and ways. This here schoolhouse we got is old, and not nigh sizable enough, and all scrouged in so's the young-uns don't have nowheres to play but the street; but hit will make a good store-seat, and Enoch

Bickers allowed he would buy hit for sech. All hands appeared to feel like Polly Ainslee's bottom, just beyand where the forks meets, was the onliest place for a right school; and then and thar Lawyer Gentry went out and seed Polly, to ax her figger, and she allowed, if hit was for the women that had waited on her so good in the typhoid, she'd name a low price—seven hunderd dollars. And when Nathe come back, though we air pore folks, hit did n't take fifteen minutes to make up that sum, which I have got hit all sot down here on paper.

"And for my part, hit was my wish not only to help a leetle with the land, but to furnish the timber for the houses; for though I am lacking in money, across yander in my hills is a sight of the finest yallow poplars the old earth ever brung forth. And when I spoke that, hit was on the lips of nigh every man present to offer his labor to cut the timber, or snake down the logs, or hew and notch 'em, or to raise the houses, or rive the boards for the roof; so you might say the buildings hain't aiming to cost no great.

"And this hain't quite all. If my land yander across Troublesome had been right land for a school, I would have give hit outright for the purpose that is most nighest my heart. But you can all see what hit is—I have deeded off passel atter passel to my offsprings as they married, till what is left is nigh straight up and down, and hain't got even a good house-seat left on hit. But I now offer to deed every foot I got left to the women, to use soon as I am dead and gone, which naturely can't be long, axing them only to let me and my old woman stay on hit till then, and have the use of the cleared land to raise corn for us and our property. All the timber and the coal to be theirn from the start, which both'll be enough to last 'em fifty year, even if the school grows like I hope hit will.

"For this is my idee, friends—that not only the young-uns in this town is to have the benefits, but that some way may be thought up so all the sprightly, ambitious-minded boys and gals in the county will get a chance at the bread of knowledge. When I let my mind run out over these mountains, and think of the dozens of young-uns up nigh every hollow, and the scores up every branch, and the hunderds—thousands, sometimes, if hit is a long one—along every creek, all with just as good, bright, hungry minds as anybody's children on earth, and all starved of their rights, half, maybe, being beyand the reach of any school, and them that goes to district school housed, maybe, worse than cattle, with the chinking all out of the walls, and the boards rotted on the roofs, and the rain a-pouring and the wind a-blowing through, and the teacher, likely, a wild boy that hain't got neither larning nor manners—why hit stirs my soul so I hain't hardly able to hold myself under.

"People, every one of our young-uns ought to have a fair chance; and hit's our business, yourn and mine, to get hit for 'em, and hit's shame and disgrace and everlasting destruction to us if we don't. And I don't see no reason why, if these women was to take pity-sake on us and come, and if we was to all pull together, and put up houses, and fetch in the young-uns, and then fetch along things for 'em to eat,— for there hain't none of us so bad off as to lack for food; there hain't a man-person here that could n't spare a wagon-load of corn and beans and 'taters for every child he brings,—and if the young-uns that comes was to do their part and work reg'lar,—for I hain't got no use for larning that sp'iles folks for work,—the boys raising gyardens and cattle and hogs and sech, for the women, and the gals cooking and cleaning, and sewing,—why I don't see no reason on earth to keep us from having a right school here. Of course, I hain't a knowledgeable man, and hain't acquainted with the workings of schools, and may be mistaken in my idees. But Amy and Virginny, you know—how does hit look to you?"

"I see what you mean, Uncle Ephraim: you plan for a school in which both brain and hand shall be trained," replied Virginia. "Certainly that is the kind of school we should wish to have, if we came. But do you realize that we are not school-teachers, that neither of us has ever taught school in her life, or would know how to go about it?"

"Maybe not, but you would know how to get them that would," replied the old man, shrewdly.

"We see the great need," said Amy, with feeling, "and should love to give our lives to filling it, if we could see the way clear. One thing you fail to realize is that such a school would require, not only the land and timber and labor and food so generously offered, but a considerable amount of money to keep it running. The only way for us to get this would be to go out into the world and tell of the needs here. Would you, and the people of the county, be willing that we should?"

Uncle Ephraim was silent a moment. Then he spoke. "We air a proud race," he said, "and like better to do for ourselves and our off-springs. But we air also pore, so far as money goes, which hain't nothing, I take hit, to be ashamed of. What we hain't noway able to do ourselves, I allow we would n't be mean enough to stand in the way of our childern getting."

"We should like to have a general expression of opinion about this," said Amy.

One after another of the leading men rose then, and concurred with Uncle Ephraim. Uncle Lot's speech was characteristic:—

"Hit allus did, and still does, go again' the grain with me to take a favor from anybody," he said, grimly; "which I allow is the drugs and settlings of cyarnality and the Old Adam still remaining in my natur.' When the Good Book declars hit is more blesseder to give than to receive, hit means what hit says; and that them that hain't got ought to humble their pride, and give them that has, a chance to bless theirselves. I hope we will all try to look at hit that way.

"And as for these women theirselves, I will say as I said down yander in the courthouse, when they first come up here I follered Solomon's counsel about strange women, and suspicioned everything they done. But I hain't seed a single thing but good come from their being with us: times is bettered, peace has lit like a dove upon us, the young has got knowledge and civility, and the old, enjoyment (which I don't hold hit's again' the will of God for us to take, in measure); and even their Sunday Schools, which some has reviled scand 'lous, I will say this much for, that, if Scripter hain't for 'em, neither is hit again' em."

"You see, women," said Uncle Ephraim, after all the others had spoken, "what the sense of the county is. If ever folks was needed and wanted and demanded, you women air, and any way you want to do will pleasure us. Say what you will, do what you will. But before we go furder with plans and arrangements, there is one more thing to tend to, right now.

"We could n't noway have the face to ax you to stay, women, on-less we could gorrontee you peace from wars and sech troubles. We all ricollect the truce that was called here in early summer by Fallons and Kents for the time you stayed. Now I could take advantage of

Fult and Darcy and say to 'em that, now you aim maybe to stay for good, the truce will hold for all time. But this would n't be hardly fair, when their intentions was only for the summer. If they will agree now, of their own free will, to make hit stand allus, then we will know just where we are at, and whether to go on and fix for the school. If they won't, then we cast our plans to the winds, dig graves for all our bright hopes, and bid you a sad far'well. Hit all hangs upon the mind of them two boys, and I ax them to be pondering whilst I talk on.

"Hit appears to me, people, that what we need is to get back to the time, two year gone, when we was enjoying peace, and when Fulty, having fit for his country, first come back from Cuby, and everybody was proud to welcome back such a pretty, brave boy; for, like his paw, he was allus much beloved. Hit is my opinion that, if he felt like working off his sperrits a leetle, then, and shooting up the town, and a few meetings, and sech-like harmless pleasures, no notice ought to have been took; hit was naetural, especially atter that turrible, pent-up year at Frankfort. The grand jury would have done better—yes, hit would, Lot—to take no notice. Atter hit did take notice, and drawed up the indictments, then Darcy, being sheriff, was obligated, whether he liked hit or not, to sarve 'em, which, as might have been foreseed, Fulty would n't stand for. So, as you mought say, the grand jury was the main cause—yes, hit was, Lot—of the war starting up again, and of placing them two boys in a position where they purely had to fight. And, not larning wisdom from experience, hit went on drawing indictments every court, which was but throwing fire in gunpowder.

"Now, my idee is to go back and drap out them two years like they had never been, and ondo what harm was done the best we can. And to that eend," drawing a sheaf of papers from his pocket, "I tuck hit upon me afore I come up here to go to the clerk's office and get out every indictment again' Fulty, which I now hold all and sing'lar here in my hand, my notion being, since they have fotched so much sorrow and trouble on us, to destroy and burn 'em here in the eyes of the county."

Calmly drawing a match from his pocket, the old man set fire to a corner of the sheaf, and held it out before him as the flames arose.

"Some folks, especially lawyers, mought say hit was a leetle high-minded for a man to take the law in his hands this way," he remarked; "but there's times, people, when righteousness has first claims over law. Hit is my prayer," he continued, watching the flames, "that in this here smoke all ricollections of Fult's and Darcy's troubles, and of their fathers' troubles afore them, shall pass away and perish."

When he had seen the last bit of paper fall to the ground and blacken and crumble, he turned to Fult.

"Fulty," he said, "Knott County hain't got ary single thing again' you no more—all is wiped out and done away. Hit confidences you never to do no more wrong.

"And you, Darcy, hain't obligated never no more to pursue atter Fult. Hit is my belief you allus wanted peace, and want it wusser now that things has come into your life to make hit more sweeter to you.

"And now I will ax you two boys to come forward here on the stand and say what you feel to do."

The two young men, both still in their lordly velvet garments, stepped on the platform from different sides, and slowly approached Uncle Ephraim and the women in the centre.

"You being the oldest, speak first, Darcy," he commanded.

Darcy, gazing all the time into the eyes of the cooking teacher below, spoke clearly, calmly. "I say let the truce hold forever," he said; "I never wanted war."

Uncle Ephraim turned to Fult. "Hit is my prayer, Fulty," he said, "that you will be of the same mind. Hit is my hope to see you from now on leading the county in goodness and rightness, and raising up offsprings for us as brave as you and as fair as Lethie here, who is our fairest."

Fult stood a moment silent. Lethie, still a fairy princess, but with little Madison now in her lap, leaned forward slightly from a front seat, her soul in her eyes as she gazed upon Fult; and Aunt Ailsie waited for his words with trembling hands.

Then he spoke. "I love my country," he said, "the land that give me birth and suck. And I love my people, though they hain't allus done me right, and some of 'em sont me off once where I could n't never see nothing but stone walls. But I don't hold that again' em—they never knowed how hard hit would be. But there is feelings in my heart I don't never expect to be able to forget, and hit was them I had to study on before I could answer Uncle Ephraim. If anything could make me forget, hit would be what he said and done here to-day; if anything could make me like the name of Kent, hit would be his goodness and justice. And I don't feel to disapp'int the hopes and expectations of that good old man, or to stand in the way of good coming to the young of this country. I will, therefore, bury my feelings as deep as I can, and give my word never to let them get the better of me no more. If I find they are aiming to bust forth, whether or no, I will quit the country before they do. I give you my hand on hit, Uncle Ephraim."

The old man took Fult's hand, with a sudden movement clasped it to his bosom, and then passed it, and afterward Darcy's, to the two women.

"You'll come to us now, women?" he asked.

Their faces bore the look of those who have just received a great and solemn call. "We will come," they answered.

Then, bowing his head upon his breast, Uncle Ephraim prayed, simply:—

"Father of our sperrits, look down upon this here scene to-day and pour out blessings upon these two young men that has put aside their hate and revengement for the good of the county; may they have a failable ricollection for meanness done 'em in the past, and hearts more and more mellered by love and life in the future. And look upon these good women, that is about to cast in their lot with us; hold up their hands while they do for our young-uns and lighten our darkness. Look upon the county, strike off hits shackles, turn again hits captivity, bring hit into the fair and wealthy land that now stretches plain in view ahead. And, Lord of all mercy, Answerer of Prayer, now lettest Thou thy servant depart in peace."